# Kane's azure eyes wandered over Janie's face lazily.

She took a deep silent breath as the subtle magnetism that was an integral part of his makeup reached out to her. His face had carved into its harsh lines a cynical sensuality that was savagely attractive, but there was more to his appeal than mere looks. He was walking dynamite—and she knew nothing at all about explosives.

"Why bother, Mr Steel?" she asked with as much acidity as she could muster. "I'm just your average working girl. There's nothing special about me."

"Wrong." His cool arrogance was incredibly infuriating.

She shrugged as casually as she could, considering he was far too close for comfort. "Most people would disagree with you," she said shortly.

"Then most people are fools."

**HELEN BROOKS** lives in Northamptonshire and is married with three children. As she is a committed Christian, busy housewife and mother, her spare time is at a premium, but her hobbies include reading, swimming, gardening and walking her two energetic, inquisitive and very endearing young dogs. Her long-cherished aspiration to write became a reality when she put pen to paper on reaching the age of forty, and sent the result off to Mills & Boon.

Look out for her next book in Harlequin Presents®, *Christmas At His Command* on sale in December.

*Books by Helen Brooks*

HARLEQUIN PRESENTS®
2153—THE MISTRESS CONTRACT

# Web of Darkness

## HELEN BROOKS

## THE MILLIONAIRES

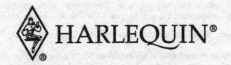

# HARLEQUIN®

TORONTO • NEW YORK • LONDON
AMSTERDAM • PARIS • SYDNEY • HAMBURG
STOCKHOLM • ATHENS • TOKYO • MILAN • MADRID
PRAGUE • WARSAW • BUDAPEST • AUCKLAND

ISBN 0-373-80515-2

WEB OF DARKNESS

First North American Publication 2002.

Copyright © 1994 by Helen Brooks.

Visit us at www.eHarlequin.com

**Printed in U.S.A.**

# CHAPTER ONE

"Joe? That man over there, the one that's just come in with the blonde woman, who is he?"

"Where?" As Joe turned round to follow the line of her eyes, he took in the general entourage surrounding the tall, powerfully built man standing in the hotel foyer, and the slender young blonde hanging like a limpet on his arm, with a wry smile.

"Oh, that's Kane Steel, sweetheart. You know, the big property tycoon who owns half of London? He's probably here for a Press conference. I wondered what all those reporters were doing hanging around. He's just pulled off one of the biggest mergers ever and the tabloids are greedy for information. Anyway, can we concentrate on the business in hand?"

As Joe turned back to the advertising material spread over the low table where they were sitting having coffee, Janie continued staring through the thin layer of glass separating the coffee-lounge from the foyer. She had known it was him! She had only seen his photo once before when she had been sorting through some of her father's papers the week after his death, but every feature of that cruel, hard face was burnt into her brain with the force of her hatred. And now he was here. In the flesh. And what was she going to do about it?

What indeed? She found she couldn't take her eyes off the huge figure as he stepped into the lift, disappearing from sight as the doors closed swiftly behind him. She had made a vow to herself, standing in the pouring rain at her father's funeral, that if she ever met the revered head of Steel Enterprises he would get what was coming to him. She just hadn't anticipated the meeting occurring in one of London's most exclusive hotels during a Press conference.

Still, what can I lose? she asked herself silently. Probably her job, the tiny flat that went with it and most of her friends, she answered mutely with cold humour. Joe Flanders was a boss in a million, but he wasn't going to like this at all and no one, *no one* crossed the great machine of Steel Enterprises, let alone the main man. Except her? The thought put iron in her backbone and fire in her eyes. She'd never sleep again at night if she didn't follow this through. She owed it to herself as well as the mild-tempered man who had given her life.

"Janie?" Joe's touch on her arm brought her eyes snapping back to him and his face straightened at the expression on hers. "What is it? Do you feel ill?"

"I'm sorry, Joe." She was already rising as she spoke. "I'll be back in a minute. There's something I have to do."

"We're meeting the manager at five, in his office," Joe said anxiously as he glanced at his watch, "and I still want to discuss these photos in more detail. Hurry up, will you? The Ladies is to the right.''

''OK.'' Once outside in the foyer, she walked straight past the powder-room and over to the large reception desk, keeping her face straight and businesslike.

''Mr Steel?'' she asked carefully. ''I understand he's holding a Press conference and I'm afraid I'm a little late. Perhaps you could direct me...?''

''Third floor,'' the girl behind the desk said in a bored tone. ''The conference-room is to your right as you step out of the lift.''

''Thanks.'' Janie's heart was beginning to thud like a piston now, but she was in the lift and out at the third floor before the trembling in her legs really took hold. She heard the noise first and, as she quietly opened the door and slipped into the large, richly carpeted room, her eyes swung immediately to the little group seated at the far end behind a magnificent desk of varnished walnut which was positioned on a small raised platform.

''Can you tell us how much the deal is worth, Mr Steel?'' one of the reporters crowding the room bellowed in her ear as Janie edged her way to the front amid a field of flashing cameras. His reply was lost on her as she reached the brief area of space before the platform. Anyone watching would have seen a rather small girl, a little inclined to plumpness, her dark hair and eyes probably her best features, with a small heart-shaped face that was averagely pretty, no more. What Kane Steel saw, as she moved to stand directly in front of him, was two blazing eyes in a dead-white face that were filled with such bitter enmity that they froze the practised reply he had been about to make and narrowed his blue eyes into cold slits.

"Mr Steel? Mr Kane Steel?" The words were piercingly clear and the silence that had gripped the little group on the platform spread in a rippling motion over the rest of the room as the hardened warriors of the Press sensed an unexpected bonus.

"Yes?" His eyes flashed over her face with devastating thoroughness. "I'm sorry, I don't know you, do I?" Someone edged forward in the watching tableau as the room held its breath, all the journalists craning their heads, notebooks ready.

"Not exactly." The bitterness was so fierce that she found she was actually having a job to speak. "But I know *you*, Mr Steel. I have good reason to know you."

"Would you like to be more explicit?" he asked icily as he rose and walked round the table, stepping down beside her on the carpet as he gestured for the others at the table to be still.

"Yes, I would." She stared up at him furiously, her cheeks scarlet. "My name is Janie Gordon, Mr Steel. My father was Paul Gordon. Ring any bells?"

"Bell-ringing is not my forte, Miss Gordon," he said coldly, "and I do not appreciate your version of *What's My Line?* in the middle of a busy work schedule. If you have something to say to me then get on with it.'' The frosty eyes dared her to continue. ''Otherwise get out.''

For a moment the sheer arrogance of the man took her breath away, and then the biting rage that had swamped her two years ago returned in all its deadly savagery.

''You are a murderer, Mr Steel.'' The hiss of indrawn breath that swept round the room was lost on her; she was blind and deaf to anything but the stone-hard face in front of her. ''A cold-blooded, despicable brute. You hounded my father for the sake of a few thousand pounds, which must be a drop in the ocean to you, until he lost everything, including the will to live. What does it feel like to have a man's death on your conscience, Mr Steel, or haven't you even thought about it?'' The vivid spots of colour burning her cheekbones brought the deathly whiteness of the rest of her face into even more stark contrast and no one could doubt that she meant every word she said.

''Miss Gordon, you are way out of line.'' There was a dangerous softness in the deep voice that spoke of furious anger. ''I have never even heard of your father—''

''Jessdon Labelling?'' She ought to be feeling intimidated, a tiny detached part of her brain thought vaguely, but, surprisingly, she felt nothing but pain, anger and relief—relief at being able to let it all out at long last. ''He named the firm after my mother,'' she added tightly. ''Jessica Gordon.''

She saw a tiny spark of awareness flare in the icy blue eyes and in the next instant her hand connected with his face with such force that his head shot back a couple of inches. As all hell broke loose behind her, the barrage of flash bulbs vying with the shouts and calls of the reporters, Janie plunged into the centre of the mêlée, forcing her way through with sheer physical force and reaching the lift outside the room just as the doors began to close. As they slid together she was aware of a tumult of bodies cascading into the corridor, the sound of raised voices fading as the lift took her swiftly downwards.

Once in the foyer, she walked rapidly out of the building, glancing neither left nor right, her eyes fixed straight ahead and her face as white as snow.

He had had it coming. He had had it coming. She continued walking blindly outside as her head swam and her mind buzzed dazedly. He was less than human, not even fit to be called an animal, and she didn't regret a thing, not a thing! The bite of cold, crisp air that carried a hint of frost in its wintry chill brought her back to reality and she suddenly realised she needed to get off the main thoroughfare in which the hotel was situated and down one of the side-streets, fast. The bloodhounds would be after her within minutes and she couldn't face anyone now. In fact, she was shaking so much she could barely stand upright.

The small wine bar halfway down the narrow road that led off the main street with its flowing traffic and bright lights was almost deserted, and as she caught the surprised eyes of the young barman it dawned on her that her coat and handbag were back with Joe at the hotel, her thin wool dress patently unsuitable for outdoor wear.

Damn, damn, damn... Once through the door trendily marked "Lassies", she leant against the cool, tiled walls of the cloakroom as her head spun. She'd have to ask the barman if she could use the phone. Maybe call the hotel and ask Joe to bring her things here? She shut her eyes tightly. He'd be furious, more than furious, but there was nothing else she could do. Even her doorkey was in that bag.

The phone call was even worse than she had anticipated, Joe's voice tight and strange-sounding, but he promised to be with her within minutes and that was all she cared about. She sat shivering slightly, more with reaction than cold, in a small alcove next to the door as the full awareness of what she had done washed over her in a sickening flood. Her father would have been horrified at his only offspring causing such a scene. She shook her head painfully as she pictured his mild, gentle face in her mind. He had been so trusting, so kind, the perfect victim for someone as ruthless as Kane Steel: the proverbial lamb to the slaughter.

"Miss Gordon?" She froze for an endless moment before turning her head with a feeling of indescribable doom as the hated voice spoke from the doorway. "You don't get away as easily as that. Outside, now!" She had never actually seen anyone's face black with rage before, but she was seeing it now, every feature twisted almost out of recognition by the violent fury that had suffused his flesh with dark colour.

"What—?" As he pulled her to her feet her voice was cut off with the speed with which he propelled her through the door. Just outside, parked more on the pavement than the road, a poker-faced chauffeur sat silently at the wheel of a magnificent silver-grey Bentley, his immaculate uniform the exact same shade as the car and his eyes staring straight ahead as Kane Steel gestured angrily towards the vehicle.

"Get in."

"You must be joking." She struggled slightly in his iron grasp, ready to make a run for it at the slightest opportunity.

"I said get in, Miss Gordon." The tone was astringent in the extreme.

"I heard you." She tried to stop the fear that was making her heart pound like a drum from showing either in her face or voice, but was aware, with humiliating chagrin, that he could probably feel the trembling that was consuming her body through his rigid hold on her arm. There wasn't a soul about. She glanced quickly up and down the deserted, discreetly lit street as icy little shivers flickered down her spine and the palms of her hands became damp with panic. Help, where was Joe; where was *anybody*? She could see the bright lights and heavy flow of traffic at the junction of the road, but here, in this quiet little backwater, all was macabrely still.

"If you are hoping Joe Flanders is coming to your rescue, forget it." He swung her round now so that she was forced to stare up into the ruthless face. "Look in there."

She glanced through the open door of the Bentley to see her coat and handbag resting on the seat. "Oh, great." There was a wealth of bitterness in her voice. "How did you manage that? Used a bit of the power and influence that makes you think you are a little tin god, I suppose?" How could Joe let her down like this? How *could* he?

"Exactly," he said bitingly. "I have met Mr Flanders on more than one occasion and he was kind enough to come forward when my assistant made enquiries at Reception and asked for your name to be broadcast just as you phoned. He knows me—"

"I *know* you," she interrupted shakily, "and that's precisely why I'm not getting in there with you."

"Think again." His smile was more like a snarl, the finely shaped lips drawing back over white strong teeth menacingly. "You are verging on charges of defamation of character, assault, causing an affray in a public place. Need I go on?" The blue eyes were merciless. "A women's prison is not the best place to spend Christmas, Miss Gordon, but it can be arranged, if you insist."

"You wouldn't..." As she stared up into the hard face her deep brown eyes widened with horror as she saw the coldness in his narrowed blue gaze. "You would, you'd actually do that?"

"Too true." He let go of her arm abruptly, sliding into the shadowed depths of the car as he left her standing, trembling, on the pavement. "You have a choice, Miss Gordon, and you will make it in the next ten seconds. You can either get in this vehicle so we can discuss your outrageous behaviour privately, or we can let the whole matter be put in the hands of officialdom. Which is it to be?'' The deep voice was merciless.

She gnawed her lower lip for a second as she stood shivering in the cold evening air. ''Where are you going to take me?''

''That's my business.'' He leant forward to fix her with the piercing eyes. ''Time's up, Miss Gordon, no more sweet persuasion.''

''You leave me with no choice,'' she said bleakly, flinching as he laughed harshly.

''Dead right.'' He moved over to the opposite side of the car as she clambered in miserably, and as she sank back she was immediately enveloped in the deliciously expensive smell of fine leather, discreetly exclusive aftershave and the unmistakable aura of fabulous wealth. ''Now.'' In the close confines of the car he suddenly seemed enormously big and for the first time her senses registered the exceptionally broad shoulders, well-developed chest and sheer breadth that went with extreme height. ''Are you going to give me your address?''

''No.'' She forced herself to look full into the rugged dark face. ''I am not.''

''Very well.'' He turned his head and spoke to the driver, giving an address she had never heard of, before snapping the glass partition shut with a definite click. ''Don't forget, I did ask,'' he drawled sardonically.

''Now just hang on a minute.'' The apprehension

and fear she had been trying to hide for the last five minutes burst forth. "You can't kidnap me."

"Kidnap you, Miss Gordon?" The firm lips drew back in an unmistakable sneer. "Why on earth would I want to kidnap such a disagreeable, patently unstable person as yourself? I have enough aggravation in my life without seeking more."

"Where are we going, then?" She ignored the insults for the moment; there were more important things to hand.

"You'll find out soon enough." He settled back in the luxurious seat and closed his eyes. "I have had just about all I am going to take tonight so I suggest you keep that nasty little mouth closed until we reach our destination. Why I am even bothering to try and find out what this is all about I don't know. I must be mad."

"You know what—"

"Be quiet, Miss Gordon." He didn't open his eyes as he spoke but the tone was enough to shut her mouth with a little snap. He was formidable. Her heart thumped against her chest wall so hard she was sure he must hear it. He was powerful and dangerous, and the sudden realisation that she had grabbed a tiger by the tail drove all lucid thought from her head for a few minutes as sheer panic had her glancing desperately out of the car window. Could she jump out at the next traffic lights? He couldn't exactly chase her through the streets of London.

"Baines has locked the doors automatically, on my instructions." The deep, gravelly voice made her jump and as her eyes shot to his face she saw that the eyelids were still firmly closed. "Lie back and enjoy the ride, Miss Gordon. You are in my clutches now, whether you like it or not."

"I don't!"

"Good." He shifted slightly as he spoke. "Consider it a down payment on your penance."

"My penance?" she squeaked disbelievingly. "Now just look here; I don't know what you've got in mind but—"

"That's probably just as well." He was quite unmoved, lying back in the seat like a great, dangerous black cat. "No one crosses me and gets away with it, Miss Gordon. Bear that in mind."

She glared at him silently as the car sped on in the night traffic, although it was quite wasted on the closed eyes. He was a very masculine man. Her gaze idly wandered over the rugged, hard features and thick, straight black hair that had touches of silver above the ears. Strong, vigorous, probably very virile…

She stiffened with horror at the path her thoughts had traversed on to. What on earth was she thinking? She couldn't care less if he was the most virile man on earth—this was Kane Steel, the original rat on two legs. So what if he was handsome? She loathed him, hated him… But then he wasn't really handsome, was he? She found herself contemplating the relaxed face again. No, not at all, really, and yet there was something, a magnetism, a breathtakingly dynamic attractiveness, that was all male and more compelling than any pretty-boy looks. She shook her head at her own treachery. There was *nothing* good about this man, nothing at all, be it looks or anything else.

As the big car ate up the miles she began to feel more and more worried with each passing landmark. This was ridiculous, absolutely ridiculous. If they didn't stop soon she would start screaming and banging on the glass partition until the driver stopped. She was a grown woman of twenty-four years of age, for goodness' sake, not some skittery schoolgirl who couldn't say boo to a goose.

"Had you eaten?"

"What?" She started so violently as the deep voice spoke that she completely missed what he had said.

The amazingly compelling eyes opened and fixed her with their arctic blueness. "I asked if you had eaten. Before your wonderful performance in front of Wapping's finest."

"It wasn't a performance, it was..." Her voice trailed away as she couldn't think of a suitable comparison and she stiffened in outrage as he smiled coldly, his face full of burningly acidic contempt.

"I am not surprised your actions leave you speechless," he said with icy biting humour. "I can assure you they had exactly the same effect on me."

"Huh!" She eyed him balefully. "Well—"

"I said, had you eaten?" There was a note in the resonant voice now that suggested she had better reply, fast.

"No, as a matter of fact," she said tightly, her eyes

flashing her hostility and dislike. "Although what it's got to do with you—"

"Spare me." He cut off her words with an irritable wave of his hand as he turned to look out of the window. "We're here."

"Where's here?" she asked warily, her gaze widening as the beautiful car drove between two wide-open gates set in a high brick wall and journeyed on down a huge gravel drive towards an enormous house in the distance.

"My home." He eyed her blandly as vivid colour surged into her cheeks. "The place where my word is law and I'm obeyed implicitly, understand?" His eyes mocked her fear.

"Your home?" Her voice had risen in line with her apprehension. "Look, I don't know what you're playing at but—"

"I am *playing* at nothing, Miss Gordon," he bit back sharply, his eyes as cold as ice and his face stony. "The last thing on my mind is games. I have been assaulted with no warning, accused of all manner of diverse crimes, forced to leave a Press conference in the worst possible circumstances, knowing that my photo will be splashed all over the front pages tomorrow morning, to the delight of my competitors, all because *you* have had a brainstorm. Now, if that counts as playing in your book you are crazier than I imagined."

"I am not crazy—" She stopped abruptly when he uncoiled his big body as the chauffeur opened the door, and he reached in as soon as he was outside, almost hauling her out of the car.

"Now you are going to come in the house and explain to me what this is all about," he said coldly, "and you'd better pray while you're about it that you can convince me it's justified."

"You're a bully," she said weakly as she stood next to him on the driveway in front of the endless mansion. She didn't know which intimidated her more, the huge, incredibly beautiful house or the massive figure next to her. At the hotel she had been too incensed and blind with rage to take in his great height, but now she realised he must be at least a foot taller than her five feet four and he towered over her like an avenging angel. Or perhaps not an angel, she corrected herself silently as her gaze fastened on the lethal cold eyes—no, definitely not!

"You don't know the half," he said grimly as he ushered her up the massive stone steps towards the crested front door. "You made me lose my temper tonight, Miss Gordon, and that's something I haven't done in years. You wouldn't like it a second time."

"No?" She stared at him defiantly as her legs shook.

"No," he said slowly, "but I've got the most distinct feeling it's a definite possibility, so just play it cool, eh?"

"Cool?" She jerked her arm from his hand and glared up into the dark face with all the venom she could muster. "Cool! You've got a cheek, you really have—"

"Now that is a clear case of the pot calling the kettle black," he said tightly as the chauffeur drove the big car past them and towards a large row of garages in the distance, "but I've got no intention of standing out here bandying words with you any more. You'll come in, you'll sit down and you will tell me what this is all about. Got it?"

As he opened the front door she had the strangest feeling, for a brief moment, that she had stepped on to the set of a film. If a famous film star had suddenly glided down the huge winding staircase that dominated the far end of the massive hall she wouldn't have been at all surprised. *Dallas* and *Dynasty*, eat your heart out, she thought with desperate humour as her eyes took in the ankle-deep cream carpet, the dark wood and obvious antiques and the glittering chandeliers overhead. And she had hit him! She had never suffered from hysteria before, but there was something flooding into her system that must be akin to it.

"In here." He had guided her across the enormous expanse and through an open door before she realised what was happening, and she found herself in a room that would have graced any stately home. "Sit down." She sank gratefully into the chair, which immediately dwarfed her small shape in its vastness; her legs had been beginning to give way. "Would you like a drink?" he asked expressionlessly.

"I'm sorry?" She dragged her eyes away from the beautifully furnished room with some difficulty and gazed vacantly at his dark face as he gestured towards a large drinks cabinet at one side of the massive fire-place.

"A drink?" he asked irritably.

She nodded tightly, her face chary. "Sherry, please, but I'm not stopping here long. I'll get a taxi home."

He poured a stiff measure of Scotch into a heavy crystal tumbler and what looked like half a bottle of pale cream sherry into a large schooner glass and walked over to her, handing her the drink before seating himself in the large armchair opposite which hardly looked big enough to hold his broad shape. All this wealth, all this luxury; how much of it had been obtained by wrecking people's lives the way he had theirs? she wondered suddenly, with a surge of anger. Driving desperate businessmen to the limit, calling in creditors, withholding loans, refusing time extensions... The list was endless and no doubt he knew all the tricks.

"OK, the spark is back in those brown eyes," he said softly. "Let's have it all, and from the beginning, please."

"What's the point?" She took a gulp of the sherry and tried to fight back the flood of emotion that was threatening to take her over. All this money—her father's little firm had been a drop in the ocean to him!

"The *point* is you made some pretty serious accusations tonight," he said furiously. "Planned to give me maximum aggravation. Now that smells bad to me, my pretty. What are you after?"

"After!" She spat the word at him as she set the sherry glass down with a bang on the little table next to the chair and stood up in a jerky movement to pace over to the crackling fire. She was cold, so cold, she'd never be warm again. She shivered violently. And she *hated* this man.

"Here." He rose quickly when he noticed the convulsive movement as the warmth flicked her frozen nerves. "I didn't give you your coat, did I? It's still in the car." As she felt the heavy material of his suit jacket slide over her shoulders she stiffened in protest. The cloth was impregnated with the clean, sensual smell of him and she didn't want it near her.

"I don't want it." She shrugged the jacket off her shoulders and handed it back to him abruptly, her eyes dark in the whiteness of her face.

His eyes narrowed as he took the coat from her and she knew he sensed her revulsion of any contact with him. It was there in the stiffening of the hard square jaw and the faintly cruel tightening of the firm mouth. That raw, almost tangible fascination was back in full force, she noted despairingly, the wide, powerful set of his shoulders more accentuated now under the silky blue shirt he wore easily, his hard masculine body taut and still as he stared down at her without speaking for long, tight seconds.

"You're pushing me to the limit," he said at last in hard, measured tones. "I don't make idle threats, Miss Gordon. I don't want to hurt you, but—"

"Hurt me?" It would have been funny if it hadn't been so painfully sad, she thought bitterly as she surveyed him through eyes misted with hot tears. "*Hurt me*? You can't do anything to me that you haven't

already done, Mr Steel,'' she said shakily as she strove
to maintain her grip on herself. ''Your ruthless greed
lost my father his business, his home and ultimately
his life. Everything is gone, everything. You have effectively wiped out the first twenty-two years of my
life. How could you follow that?'' She pushed back
her heavy fold of silky black hair from her shoulders
with a trembling hand as she spoke. ''And the worst
thing of all is that you didn't even remember his
name.''

The tears that had been threatening to overflow all
night wouldn't be denied any longer and, as she lowered her head blindly, her cheeks wet with the warm,
salty flow, she realised, with a stab of horror, that she
was going to make an even worse fool of herself than
she had already. And there wasn't a thing she could
do about it, not a thing.

# CHAPTER TWO

QUITE how she found herself cradled in the strong, hard arms Janie never did know, but the big masculine chest was incredibly comforting as she howled out her misery, in spite of it belonging to the perpetrator of all the pain.

When the tempest had ceased and her weeping had died to the odd hiccuping sob, he put her firmly to one side.

"So your grievance is genuine," he stated expressionlessly. She glanced up at him quickly, noting that the hard blue eyes were guarded and there was a subtle change in him she couldn't quite discern. His mouth was still cruel and cynical, the deep lines grooved either side of his nose still fiercely prominent and the overall impression was still one of ruthless ferocity, and yet...there was something. "I can recognise real misery when I see it, Miss Gordon," he said slowly, "but your actions are still inexcusable. You could have made an appointment to speak with me at any time to sort out this misunderstanding—"

"Misunderstanding!" She reared up like a small tigress. "There's no misunderstanding, believe me, and you can't fool me like that either; I'm not stupid."

"I won't make the obvious retort to that statement," he said coldly. "Your actions speak far louder than any words of mine could do. How long has it been since your father died?" he finished abruptly.

"Two years." She stared at him tightly.

"Did you cry when he died?" He ignored the painful tensing of her body, his face demanding an answer.

"Well, of course..." Her voice trailed away as her brow puckered in thought. "No, I suppose not, not really."

"That is very bad for your soul." She stared at him in surprise. It was the last thing she had expected from a callous, harsh entrepreneur like him. "It creates a darkness, like a web, that blankets everything."

"Look, I'm fine." She straightened slightly as she spoke, her chin jutting out aggressively. "There's nothing wrong with *me*." The last words were full of meaning and he nodded slightly, his eyes hardening.

"I take it we're back to the accusations?"

"Oh, you know what I mean." She brushed a strand of hair from her damp face wearily. "You can't have forgotten so completely. I could see you remembered at the hotel."

"The name of your father's firm, that is all." She was aware as they talked, in a tiny separate little compartment in her mind, that her body was still registering the feel and smell of him as he had held her in his arms. The knowledge was painful and treacherous and altogether unwelcome, but it was there. She had never met anyone like him before. She didn't like the way he made her feel, but she couldn't do anything about it either. Every little cell in her body seemed determined to hold on to the tingling electricity his hard male shape had induced. "Look, start at the beginning; humour me."

As he walked across the room to his chair her senses registered a carefulness in his walk, almost a hesitancy, that was incongruous in such a giant of a man, but as he sat down she brushed the fancy aside irritably. He was getting under her skin for some reason and she could do without it.

"Well, there's not much to tell really." She sniffed dismally and looked across at him slowly. "Have you got a handkerchief?"

"Yes, I've got a handkerchief." He answered her in the same dull tone in which she had spoken and a burst of adrenalin put scarlet in her cheeks as he reached across with a large square of white cotton. Had she sounded like that? She'd have to watch herself—it wouldn't do for him to think he had the upper hand. And how *dared* he mock her?

"My father founded the firm with my mother the year I was born," she said quietly, after she had blown her nose and settled back in her seat. "They did quite well too—we had a nice house and the usual little luxuries. Not like this, of course—" her eyes bit at him with heavy sarcasm "—but we were happy."

"Yes?" he prompted her as she paused, her eyes cloudy with memories.

"Then my mother got ill, a heart complaint, when I was in my early teens. Dad spent more and more time with her. I don't think she knew he mortgaged the house to keep the firm going—I certainly didn't. She died just as I started university.''

"I'm sorry." The piercing blue eyes never left her face for a moment, the deep voice quite devoid of expression.

"Dad was devastated, naturally, but then he threw himself into the firm, trying to claw back the time he had lost, I guess, and he was doing quite well. We had a loyal workforce and he could spend as many hours as he wanted there now with Mum gone, which helped him actually, took his mind off things. He'd just secured a big contract which he was thrilled about; it would have made the house safe again and he wanted that for me, but then—'' She stopped abruptly and raised her eyes full on his face. "Then Steel Enterprises stepped in."

"How?" he asked grimly.

"Don't you remember?" She stared at him angrily. "It was only just over two years ago; you can't have forgotten the details so quickly."

"Do you have any idea just how vast my corporation is?" he asked tightly. "And I have other business interests abroad that take a lot of my time and attention. I can't personally get involved in everything."

"No, I suppose not." The thought hadn't occurred to her and her eyes opened wide for an instant. "Well, you—your firm," she corrected hastily, "had bought the rest of the block our small factory and office was in and you wanted our space. There was nowhere else we could go immediately—your offer was abysmally low. It was common knowledge that Dad's firm was having problems, and when Dad refused to sell you put the squeeze on."

"I see." His face was blank, almost uninterested.

"Banks suddenly foreclosed, contracts died, the whole caboodle folded in on itself." She glared at him angrily. "It's a lovely way to do business, isn't it, Mr Steel, but I suppose all is fair in love and war? That's obviously the principle you promote. Even if you yourself weren't personally overseeing this particular deal, you can't tell me your employees would go against the rules, your normal operating procedures."

"I wasn't aware I had to tell you anything," he said coldly and she flinched at the icy tone. He was talking to her, listening, but part of his mind seemed to be ticking on elsewhere. She stared at him hard. What was he thinking about? "Do continue." He leant forward slightly, the movement causing her heart to jump into her mouth as the shirt stretched tight for a moment over his broad chest. Stop it, she chided herself angrily, you're as jumpy as a kitten.

"And goodbye firm." She forced herself to speak calmly. "Goodbye house. Dad got a part-time job for a pittance and lodged with friends, and within four months he was dead. The doctor said it was pneumonia aggravated by a dose of flu, but he just gave up the will to live, that's what killed him." She stared at him painfully. "He wanted to die; he told me so."

"And you blame me for that?"

"Totally." She rose as she spoke. "My dad used to have a saying—the buck stops here. Do you know it?" She smiled grimly. "Well, the buck stopped fair and square at your door, Mr Steel, even if you aren't man enough to pick it up. Your company policies stink, your employees stink—and you stink.''

''Graphically put,'' he said sardonically.

''And that's it?'' Two bright spots of colour burnt in her cheeks as she faced him, her thick black hair shining red under the bright artificial lights, her dark brown eyes enormous. ''A touch of sarcasm while holding on to your precious dignity? No apology, no regret, no guilt?''

''I have nothing to feel guilty about.'' He too had risen, to walk across to a long bell-cord in the corner of the room which he pulled twice. Almost immediately the door opened to reveal a pretty, petite maid complete with starched apron and mob-cap. ''Could you ask Mrs Langton to step in here a moment, please, June?'' he asked smoothly. ''I'd like a word with her.''

''Yes, sir.'' The maid's big blue eyes opened wide at the sight of Janie. ''I'm sorry, sir, we didn't know you were home. We thought you were out for the evening—''

''My plans changed.'' The words were dismissive and the small girl immediately left the room with a quick, nervous nod of her head. ''I'm going to order us dinner.'' As the blue eyes fastened on Janie she stared at him in horror.

''Not for me, Mr Steel,'' she said quickly. ''I've had my say; I want to go home.''

''No way.'' His voice was curt. ''I haven't finished

with you yet, not by a long chalk, besides which I
need to check your story.''

"Not now?'' She glanced at the small gold wrist-
watch on her arm. "It's way past six on a Friday night.
There won't be anyone about.''

"There will be people about if I need them to be,''
he said coldly, "and the bare facts will be down on
record. The more detailed fill-in will have to wait until
I can find out who was in charge of that particular
deal.''

"Look, I'm going.'' She took one step towards the
door, but the rigid immobility of the big body in front
of her froze her next step. "I mean it, I want to go
home.''

"Don't be so childish.'' The shock of his words
brought the angry colour that had just died surging
back into her cheeks. "I'm just offering you dinner
while certain enquiries are made, that's all. You are
most fortunate you aren't being charged at the local
police station on various counts.''

"But your evening?'' A mental picture of the tall,
slim blonde flashed into her mind. "You obviously
intended to be out tonight and—''

"It's a little late to start concerning yourself about
my situation, don't you think?'' he asked smoothly.
"You can have another sherry while I make a few
calls and then we will eat.''

As she opened her mouth to argue the door opened.
"Mrs Langton.'' Kane Steel smiled at the stout middle-aged woman who stepped into the room, her iron-
grey hair tightly drawn back in a severe bun and her

stiff black dress looking as though it would retain its shape with or without a body inside it. "My plans have changed and I now require dinner for two. Is that possible?"

"Of course, Mr Steel." Mrs Langton smiled formally. "In half an hour?"

"Fine." As the woman left with a smile and a nod in Janie's direction, Janie glared at him angrily.

"What do I have to do to convince you that I don't want dinner?"

"Nothing, I know it already," he said imperturbably.

"Then why?"

"Because you'll do as you're told." The statement was clearly a complete answer as far as he was concerned and she stared at him furiously, incensed by his arrogance.

"You really are the most incredible man," she said in tones of deep disgust, her fury escalating as he smiled mockingly, his dark face alive with cruel humour. He was still angry, very angry.

"You are not the first female to say that," he said tauntingly, "although I have to admit the circumstances are a first. Normally it is said with more... enthusiasm."

"Is it indeed?" She tried to inject as much scorn and derision into her voice as she could. "I was always under the impression that a real man didn't have to boast about his performance in bed."

"Was I talking about bed?" he asked softly, with satirical coolness, but she noticed her insult had narrowed the ice-blue eyes and straightened his mouth. "You know, this business about your father apart, you really are a little shrew, aren't you? Don't you like men, Miss Janie Gordon?"

He had remembered her Christian name from the hotel. As she glared back into the rugged face the thought hammered in her brain. In spite of all the chaos and aggravation, he had remembered, and she suddenly knew it was indicative of the man himself. His mind was razor-sharp and as hard as nails; he wouldn't forget a thing, ever. So why the memory-loss regarding her father's firm? Did she believe him? Had he been involved with it all? He didn't seem the type of man to let anything slip through his fingers, least of all the knowledge of the acquisition of a prime block of real estate. He would have known an outline of the situation at least, especially in view of the difficulties involved. He would have had to, surely? And he *had* recognised the name of the firm.

"Well?" As she came back to the present he was still holding her with that rapier-sharp blue gaze.

"What?" She had lost the thread of the conversation completely.

"Men, do you like men?" He took a step towards her as she tried to concentrate on what he was saying and not her churning thoughts. "There's one way to find out…" The manner in which he folded her into his arms spoke of an expertise that only registered on Janie much later; at that precise moment she was too busy struggling against his superior strength. She found, to her fury, that she was quite helpless in his embrace. The big body was all muscled power and firm, hard flesh, and she was caught as securely as a tiny fish in a net. This was part of the penance?

As his mouth closed on hers she forced herself to stand still. Her movements were only bringing her more intimately into contact with that hard male frame, besides which resistance was useless and they both knew it. The kiss was firm and warm and sensual and she hated the excited trembling it triggered in all different parts of her body—it was a betrayal to her father and to herself. But she couldn't help it. The thought weakened her still further. What was it about him? She had never had a kiss affect her like this before.

He moved her closer into him as he allowed one hand to play up and down her back in a soothing, hypnotic rhythm that set fire alarms off all over her body. She should have felt frightened, threatened—she was at his mercy here when all was said and done—but her whole being was coping with the ripples of pleasure that were flowing through her body as he explored the contours of her mouth, his lips gentle and erotic in turn. His mouth was a sweet torture and tormentingly knowing as it wandered over her closed eyelids, her throat, her ears, creating havoc to her nervous system and a warm ache in her lower stomach as it did its devastatingly sensual work.

Then she was free and he brushed his lips lightly over hers once more before stepping back to survey her with narrowed eyes and crossed arms. "Very nice." His voice was soft and deep but for the life of her she couldn't say a word as she gazed silently back into the harsh, strong face. "Very nice indeed, and now you are going to have another drink and I am going to make some phone calls."

She was still standing in stunned silence when he left the room seconds later after filling her glass and placing it back on the table near her chair. The swine! Her legs were beginning to shake and she almost collapsed into her seat, her mind whirling, as the click of the door released her from the dazed trance. She didn't doubt for a minute that the kiss had been intended as a punishment. She groaned out loud into the empty room. She should have shouted at him when he released her, told him exactly what she thought of him, slapped his face— But she'd already done that once tonight. She shut her eyes tightly for a second. This was all a dream—it had to be; nothing else would explain the dizzy stupor his lips had evoked.

She took a big gulp of sherry as she glanced round the magnificent room again, noticing, as she did so, a photograph of two men to one side of the mantelpiece. She rose to take a closer look. It had to be Kane Steel and a brother or cousin—the likeness was uncanny, although the smaller man was of a lighter build and his hair was fairer. Nevertheless the two faces boasted an unmistakable blood tie. It must have been taken years ago, she thought idly as she looked at the much younger Kane smiling back at her. The deep lines that were grooved into his face now and the touches of grey in his hair were missing, along with the rather tense way in which he held himself.

He did look older, she thought suddenly; that was why for a moment she hadn't been sure if it was him at the hotel. The photograph that had been in her father's papers had been of a much younger man, too, although admittedly it had been the usual polished pose of a publicity shot and, consequently, remote and unlifelike. She would have to go through those papers again. After the initial tearful sorting she had bundled everything into a big box and stuffed it into a cupboard, and ever since it had been too painful to resurrect.

When he returned, ten minutes later, she was quite composed and poised, at least on the outside. Inside was a seething mass of emotion like a volcano before the lid was blown.

"Prawn cocktail and steak and salad all right?" he asked blandly as he entered the room. "With fresh peaches in brandy for dessert?" He eyed her narrowly, his face grim.

"Fine." She nodded jerkily. Get through the next couple of hours the best you can and then you're free, she told herself silently, and you needn't ever see him again. Unless it was in court, of course. No doubt the vicious take-over, the ruthless but legal destruction of all that her father had built up for years, would be explained away calmly and logically, with Steel Enterprises coming up smelling of roses. She didn't know why he was going through this farce, but that was undoubtedly what it was. Corporate giants were totally ruthless and never admitted to being in the wrong.

Rule number one. And it *had* been legal, she reminded herself again. Cruel, wicked, heinous but…legal.

As he seated himself in his chair after pouring another whisky she gestured to the photograph unsmilingly. "Your brother?"

"Yes." He followed her gaze. "That's Keith."

"He's younger than you?" she asked carefully.

"By four years." He took a long draught from his glass and settled back in his chair. "That was taken three years ago when we were on holiday in Greece."

"Three years?" She stared at him in surprise. Three years; she would have said at least ten. He read her face accurately.

"I'm thirty-four years old, Miss Gordon," he said tightly, "and my brother died last year. Can we leave the subject now?"

"Of course." She nodded quickly as her cheeks burnt hotly. How was she supposed to know his brother was dead? And she *would* have put Kane Steel at least eight or nine years older, although the lean, hard body was ageless. It was that devastatingly attractive face that had fooled her. What had happened to put those lines round his mouth and eyes? It must have been something catastrophic to have made such a difference in three years? His brother's death maybe? Or was there something else?

The dinner was excellent, but the huge ornate room in which it was served was daunting, to say the least. When Kane first led her into it she took a deep breath and prayed for aplomb; the massive dark wood dining-table, thick white carpet and cream-textured walls, combined with the heavy velvet drapes in a dark rich burgundy, were grandly intimidating, and it was *colossal*.

"Do you always eat in here?" she asked him quietly as June cleared the dinner-plates from the table preparatory to dessert. The whole meal had been conducted in tight, painful silence.

"When I have guests." He looked at her closely. "Don't you like this room?"

"Where do you eat when you don't have guests?" she prevaricated quickly.

"In my study," he said shortly. "In fact I spend most of my time in this house in there. Do you want to eat dessert in the study?" he asked suddenly.

"Yes, please," she said instantly.

He blinked and looked round the dining-room bewilderedly. "What's wrong with it?"

"Nothing, it's beautiful," she said quickly, "but it's just so big! Well, let's face it, it's gigantic."

"Is it?" He glanced round the room again. "Yes, I suppose it is really. I never think about it."

How the other half live, she thought wryly as she followed him across the vast hall into a much smaller room than the others, but one which could still have swallowed her tiny flat whole. It was cosy, though. A crackling fire was burning in the hearth, one wall was lined with books that shone dully in the subdued glow from the copper wall-lights and thick, heavy gold drapes at the window had been pulled against the cold night, giving a homely feel to the room that was accentuated by the large tabby cat curled up on the leather settee by the fire.

"You own a cat?" She hadn't put him down as an animal lover.

"Cats. This one's Juniper—there's another one, Cosmos, around somewhere," he said vaguely. As Mrs Langton and June set the small table that was tucked away in one corner of the room, Janie stroked the soft fur of the large tabby and watched Kane Steel from under her eyelashes. In spite of all her efforts to the contrary, she couldn't help remembering how it had felt to be held close to that magnificent chest. He really did have a superb body. The thought made her blush as hotly as if she had voiced it and she lowered her eyes quickly. The sooner she was out of here the better, and she had better remember that the kiss had been a male punishment, an offering to his damaged ego after the scene at the Press conference. Typical of the sort of man he was, she thought tightly. It must have hit him hard to have his dirty washing laundered in public.

The peaches in brandy, heavily doused with thick double cream, were delicious, but the sense of unreality that had been steadily growing all night intensified as they finished the dessert. "Coffee?" He looked very big and very dark in the smaller room, the piercing blueness of his eyes at odds with the tanned skin, and again the enigmatic appeal of the man reached out to her, strong and fierce, until she found her heart was pounding out of control.

"No." She stood up abruptly and walked over to the log fire. "No, thank you, I really must go."

"Why?" His voice was caustic. "I thought we were having a wonderful time." The sarcasm was bitingly cold.

"I don't see what you're so het up about," she said furiously as her temper reached boiling-point. "Now Joe Flanders knows what I've done, I've probably lost my job and my flat, not to mention my credibility. You're sitting pretty with virtue intact, aren't you? I'm the one who will be made the scapegoat."

"Made the scapegoat?" he repeated incredulously as his eyes raked over her hot face. "I don't believe I'm hearing this! Do you have any idea of what you did tonight, young woman? In the middle of a Press conference, a *Press conference*," he repeated furiously, "you accused me of being a murderer and a swindler and goodness knows what else. There isn't a journalist in London who will miss a scoop like that and I wouldn't wonder a couple of them got a nice juicy picture of your hand connecting with my face as the icing on the cake. Anything you get from Joe Flanders you deserve. To have planned something like that—"

"I didn't plan it," she said indignantly, her brown eyes flashing black sparks. "I was with Joe in the coffee-lounge—we had an appointment with the manager about some advertising work—when I saw you come in. It was an impulse thing."

He swore, softly and fluently, as he shut his eyes for a split-second. "I don't know if that makes it worse or better. Didn't you stop for a moment to think about the repercussions that were bound to follow?''

"No." She stared straight into the blue eyes. "But if I had I'd still have done exactly the same."

"Would you indeed?" His face was black with rage. "You really want a good whipping to bring you to heel, young lady."

"You touch me again, in *any* way, and *I'll* be the one bringing an assault charge," she said angrily. "Got it?"

He shook his head slowly. "You're eaten up with this."

"What do you expect?" she said fiercely as her hands clenched into fists at her side. "He was my father, not some vague acquaintance. How would you feel if someone treated your father like that?"

"Like murder," he said without a trace of amusement in his face, "but it's all supposition at the moment, isn't it? I haven't had anything confirmed and it seems to me that you've put your own interpretation on events, in any case. You don't know for sure exactly what happened on the business side and, I repeat, your behaviour is inexcusable."

"I know enough." She faced him stiffly. "More than enough, and I want to go now."

"OK, OK." He stood up slowly, almost carefully, and again she got the impression that the movement was deliberate, thought out in advance. "I'm expecting a call in half an hour; you don't want to hang around for the outcome?"

"No, I don't," she said coldly. "I know my facts

are accurate, Mr Steel, and I also know what your supposed enquiries will reveal.''

''Then you're way in front of me.'' He stared at her, his face tight and mordant. ''To be honest, I've had more than my fill of your particular brand of charm for one evening.''

''Why break the habit of a lifetime by being honest now?'' she asked bitingly, her eyes flashing sparks.

''I think I probably asked for that.'' The harsh grooves in his face deepened as he turned abruptly away. ''You don't miss an opportunity, do you? I'll have to remember that for the future.''

''Future?'' she asked with icy contempt. ''I doubt if our paths will ever cross again. Your lifestyle and mine are hardly on a par, are they?''

''Oh, you don't get off as lightly as that,'' he said coldly, his eyes lethal. ''You're wrong, Miss Gordon, and I'll prove it to you, and when it's confirmed that you've made a grave error—''

''It won't be,'' she said firmly. ''I told you what happened in the past and I'm still far from sure you aren't fully aware of it all anyway. I don't need to have what I've told you confirmed or otherwise. I *know* what happened. I'd like to go now.''

''As you wish.'' He pressed a tiny gold button at the side of the fireplace and within seconds the little maid had popped her head round the door.

Didn't he ever do anything himself? Janie thought cynically as she watched him giving orders to the small girl. Buttons for this, orders here and there, everyone jumping to attention. Her face was cryptic as he glanced back to her and the piercing gaze had swept over her features before she could school them into a more acceptable mask.

"So much hate in one small package." His voice was deep and soft and, for some reason, tiny flickers of fire shivered down her spine as he walked over to her, lifting a lock of silky black hair and rubbing it in his fingers as he looked hard into her dark brown eyes. "It's very bad for you, you know," he said mockingly, his eyes glittering coldly.

"So you said before." She flicked her head away sharply. "Did I understand that you've asked for the car to take me home? I'm quite capable of phoning for a taxi."

"I think you're quite capable of anything." There was a note in his voice she couldn't quite place, but it made the goose-bumps rise all over her body. "However, I would prefer to take you home myself, having brought you here in the first place."

"You're coming too?" Her voice was frankly dismayed and a glimmer of a smile touched the frosty face for a fleeting moment.

"I was only saying the other day to a colleague that it would be a pleasant change to meet a girl whose head wasn't turned by the Steel name," he said sardonically as he moved back to his place in front of the fire. "I forgot that little law that says we should be careful what we ask for in case we get it."

She eyed him without speaking—there was nothing she could say after all—and within sixty seconds June had returned to announce that the car was waiting at the main entrance.

As they left the beautifully warm house and stepped into the cold night, the wind blew against Janie's face with tiny chips of sleet in its arctic depths and, once in the car, she drew her coat off the seat where it was lying with her handbag and pulled it round herself gratefully.

"Cold?" He had seated himself opposite her, like before, the blue eyes watchful.

"A little." She glanced out of the dark window quickly and searched for something impersonal to say. "Where are we?"

"Middlesex," he said coldly. "The Mother of London, near enough to make travelling easy and yet still retaining country lanes with working farms and thatched cottages that would grace any village in Yorkshire."

"You're a country boy at heart?" she asked cynically as she pulled the coat still closer round her shape.

"You find that hard to believe?" he said expressionlessly. "You have me set in the North Circular Road with its attendant miles of buildings and Tube stations and so on? Or maybe in the heart of London, the West End or Chelsea?"

"I would say the latter would suit you better." She made no attempt to soften her words. "I should think the only interest you would display in villages and suchlike is in their market value."

"That is what you would say, is it?" The blue eyes

were diamond-hard. "It is a pity that such attractiveness goes hand in hand with such ignorance."

"How dare you?" She reared up like a small black kitten when confronted by a sleek, full-grown panther.

"How dare I?" His voice was deceptively mild in comparison to the steel-hard set of his jaw. "Your terminology is all wrong, Miss Gordon. It is I who should be asking you that. You know nothing about me, nothing at all, beyond the rather vague notion that I was responsible for causing your father some grief—"

"Vague?" Her voice was so shrill, he winced slightly before continuing as though she hadn't spoken.

"And you continue to be obnoxious at every turn, refusing to listen to common sense and altogether behaving in a manner more suited to an infant than a grown woman of...?" She held his glance, her mouth obstinately shut. "Twenty-three, twenty-four?" he persisted with inflexible tenacity.

"Twenty-four, not that it's any of your business," she returned sharply, "and what about your behaviour anyway?"

"My behaviour?" He lifted dark eyebrows with such haughtiness that Janie could have hit him—again. "As far as I recall, I merely gave you a lift in my car when you were coatless and hatless, so to speak, and provided you with an adequate meal. That constitutes a felony in your book?"

"I don't mean that," she said angrily, her rage flooding her system with such warmth that the coat was quite unnecessary. "I mean when you—" She stopped abruptly. "When you manhandled me," she finished tightly.

"*I* manhandled *you*?" The amazed outrage was genuine. "My head is still ringing from the contact with your hand, young lady; when the hell did I manhandle you?"

"In your drawing-room," she said flatly, "when you kissed me."

"Ah..." The word was full of meaning and her head snapped up to find the dark face was surveying her with mocking intentness. "Now you are going to try and tell me you didn't enjoy it?"

"No, I didn't!" She glared at him, almost incoherent with temper. "It was sickening, absolutely sickening. I've never been treated like that in my life."

"Really?" He settled further back in his seat, crossing his arms across his chest as the piercing eyes narrowed into blue slits of light and she realised, quite suddenly, that he was playing with her, like a sleek black cat with a tiny mouse. "The male population in general is sensible enough to have nothing to do with you? There's hope for the universe yet."

"I don't mean I've never been kissed," she said furiously, "and you know it. I mean—" She broke off. What did she mean? "To be forced—"

"Oh, come, come." He actually had the nerve to smile. "Maybe for the first moment or two, but after that?" The hard male face was maddeningly cool. "I was there, remember."

"You're a pig," she said weakly, "and I'm not dis-

cussing this with you. In fact I'm not discussing anything with you.'' She shut her eyes determinedly,
drawing the coat more tightly round her shoulders.

"I'm glad I was there," the deep voice said reflectively after a long minute had passed in silence. "I, at
least, found the experience most...rewarding." She
didn't open her eyes and several miles flashed by before he spoke again. "I'd appreciate some indication
of where we are going?"

"Oh, you can drop me anywhere." She opened her
eyes quickly and glanced out of the car window into
the steady downpour that had materialised outside.
Cocooned in the luxurious interior of the Bentley, the
world outside seemed a million miles away.

"Well, you are consistent, I'll give you that," he
said coldly. "That comment matches the rest of the
rubbish you've spoken all night. Have you noticed it's
throwing everything down out there and you are in a
thin wool dress and coat that wouldn't last a minute?
Now, an address, please."

"Aberdeen Gardens," she said after a long pause.

"And the number?"

"Sixty-two." Aberdeen Gardens was two streets
away from where her flat was situated, but she didn't
want him to know where she lived. She hadn't worked
out why yet, she just knew with deep conviction that
the less he knew about her the better. He was a threat,
a definite threat to her peace of mind, and not just
because of past history. She was used to dealing with
all sorts of men in her job as Joe Flanders' personal
secretary and could keep the most obstreperous indi-

viduals at bay with a few well-chosen, crushing remarks or careful diplomacy, but this man... She glanced at him again in the dim light from the passing street-lamps, contemplating the hard square jaw and lethal body. This man was a whole new ball game.

After he had given Baines the address, he slid the glass partition back firmly into place, shutting them once again in their own disturbingly intimate atmosphere. "Do you live alone?" The question threw her for a brief moment and she hoped he hadn't noticed.

"Yes." The one word was abrasive and curt.

"One-bedroomed flat?" He was pertinacious, she had to give him that.

"Yes." She looked out of the car window as she spoke; those eyes were hypnotic. "It's in a house Joe owns; he rents it to me as part of my job package."

"I see." He nodded slowly. "Hence the losing job, losing home comment. Have you worked for him long?"

"Ever since leaving university, just over two years." She looked into his face now. "My father died two weeks after I got my degree."

"I see." He didn't; how could he? she thought bitterly. She had been counting the days until she could leave university and get a little flat for them both, look after her father properly, spoil him a little. And then...

"Here we are, Aberdeen Gardens." As the big car nosed carefully into the secluded square of neat maisonettes, Janie breathed a silent sigh of relief. "Sixty-two?"

"Yes." She smiled coldly. "Now you can be rid of me, can't you?"

"For the moment, Miss Gordon, for the moment." As the Bentley drove round in a semicircle, she sat rigidly on the edge of her seat, waiting for the moment when she could escape. What a night, *what a night*!

"I'm sorry, sir." Baines had stopped the car with the engine running and moved the partition aside. "The numbers only go up to sixty."

"They can't do," Kane said irritably before he caught sight of her face. "But then again... Just a moment and I'll come back to you." He turned to her, his eyes icy. "Right, very cute, very cute indeed, and now we'll have the proper address. I'm too old in the tooth to play these childish games, Miss Gordon, and one more mistake like that and you'll find out what it's like to be well and truly spanked. Got it?"

"You wouldn't dare." She glared at him furiously.

"You want to bet?" There was no humour in the dark face, just pure undiluted rage. "You want taking in hand, my girl. Now, the address?"

"I can walk from here," she said obstinately and then jumped violently as he banged a fist on to the seat, snarling under his breath in the same moment.

"Give me patience!" His eyes were very blue and as sharp as glass. "I don't want to come in and tuck you into bed, Miss Gordon, I want to deliver you home to your front door, and the quicker the better as far as I'm concerned. You are easily the most troublesome female I have had to deal with in a very long time and

I have no wish to prolong this painful encounter any longer than I have to. Now—the damn *address*!''

She was aware of Baines sitting rigidly still in front and clearly able to hear every word, and as she opened her mouth to argue the futility of it all swept over her. He would persevere until he got the address and she had the feeling his will was stronger than hers, much as she hated to acknowledge it.

''It's two streets away—Meldon Court, number sixty-two,'' she said flatly as her cheeks glowed bright red.

''Are you sure?'' The sarcasm was biting.

''Yes,'' she nodded quickly. ''The number was right anyway.''

He cast a scathing glance in her direction before turning round to Baines. ''Got that?''

''Yes, sir.''

''Then get on with it; the sooner we drop this unwelcome parcel off the better.'' He slid the glass to with such force that she wouldn't have been surprised if it had shattered all over them.

Sixty seconds later they drew up outside the tall terraced house in which Janie had her flat and as Baines opened the door she was out like a shot.

''Goodbye.'' She held out her hand as Kane followed her into the street, her eyes fiery. ''I can't say it was pleasant meeting you.''

''Likewise.'' He took her hand in his, his large brown fingers burying her small hand. ''I hope for your sake the headlines are different from what I expect tomorrow,'' he said threateningly.

She had expected him to shake her hand, but as he raised it to his lips, turning the palm over at the last moment, she forced herself to stand perfectly still even as tiny little tinglings scattered through her nervous system. As his warm, firm lips connected with the soft interior of her palm, the breath stopped in her throat and then pounded down into her chest in a surge of feeling that made her quite dizzy. The brilliant blue eyes were on a level with her shocked brown ones as he raised his head after a long moment, and as he straightened she saw he wasn't smiling.

"Goodnight, Janie," he said expressionlessly.

"*Goodbye*, Mr Steel." Her voice wasn't as cool as she would have liked it to be and the knowledge was humiliating as she fumbled with the doorkey, all fingers and thumbs, stepping into the hall as the door opened and shutting the door behind her without a backward glance. She leant against the cold wall for a moment before racing up the two flights of stairs to her flat, dropping the key twice as she tried to insert it into the lock, and only feeling safe as she stumbled into her tiny home and slammed the door shut behind her.

# CHAPTER THREE

THE sense of anticlimax when Janie awoke late on Saturday morning was as unwelcome as it was unsettling. She had lain awake for half the night, her tired mind doing endless post-mortems on every word, every gesture they had exchanged until she had felt she was going mad. She was glad she had confronted him, she *was*, she told herself fiercely time and time again through the endless dark hours. All she needed to do now was to let go of it all. But she couldn't. She had thumped her pillow in helpless frustration before falling asleep as pink touched the night sky.

The shrill tone of the phone as she sat gloomily nursing a mug of scalding-hot coffee brought her heart shooting into her mouth. "Don't be so stupid," she muttered angrily to herself as she reached across the tiny breakfast-bar to pluck the phone off the wall. It wouldn't be him; of course it wouldn't be him. It wasn't.

"Janie?" Joe Flanders' voice was about as irate as she had ever heard it. "Have you seen the papers? Whatever possessed you, girl?"

"The papers?" she asked helplessly as her heart sank. "Are they bad?"

A harsh expletive followed. "The worst!" her employer barked into the phone. "Are you going to explain to me?"

"Of course." She took a deep breath. "It's a long story."

"It must be." Joe's voice was wry. "I'm just amazed you're still around to tell it."

"The phrase 'extenuating circumstances' does apply, Joe," she said weakly, "and I'm really sorry about leaving like that."

"I was worried about you," Joe said more quietly. "Very worried. I wasn't sure if I'd done the right thing in letting him have your things, but he was very insistent."

"I can imagine," she said drily. "Look, can I explain properly on Monday when I see you? And I *am* sorry, Joe, really. Don't write me off yet, please."

"I won't," he said quietly. "I'll see you at the office then, but, if you should need me before that, you've got the number."

"I know, thanks."

The weekend dragged by in spite of an invite to a rather off-beat party on Saturday night and Sunday lunch with an old schoolfriend, and by the time she arrived at the office on Monday morning she was more than glad to be back in the hurly-burly of Joe's hectic advertising agency despite the punishing pace.

She outlined the bare facts briefly to Joe before the day's work really started and was grateful when he restrained his comments to a cursory raising of his eyebrows and a shaking of his grey head. The day raced by as it always did, but even in the most chaotic moments she was aware that a tiny segment of her mind was thinking about a very tall, dark man and was exasperated with her lack of control. Would he contact her again? The thought that had been drumming in the back of her head all weekend had free rein on the bus-ride home as she sat sandwiched between two young girls who were exchanging avid gossip about a mutual acquaintance with salubrious enjoyment. She hoped not. A tiny dart of disquieting honesty pricked at the back of her mind questioningly. She *did* hope not. If she ever saw him again in the whole of her life it would be too soon. But he'd contact her. She remembered the graphic headlines in the newspapers and flinched helplessly.

The crisp knock on the door as she began to prepare her solitary meal later that evening caused a moment's panic before she spoke sternly to herself. "Calm down; you can't act like this indefinitely." It was bound to be Annie from next door asking for the spare key she kept in Janie's flat. She was always locking herself out.

As she opened the door and raised her eyes up and up to meet Kane Steel's cool, sardonic gaze, she realised she wasn't at all surprised; she had somehow known that he wouldn't be able to leave matters long—he wasn't that type of man. He would have to dot the "i"s and cross the "t"s to his own satisfaction and extract his last pound of flesh in the process.

"I've been expecting you," she said carefully through the mad pounding of her heart. "I saw the papers, too. Are you alone?'' She half expected a solicitor to pop up behind him.

''Can I come in?'' He cut through the niceties with a terse nod of his head to the room beyond.

''I guess.'' What on earth was he going to think of her tiny little flat? she thought helplessly as she gestured him into the minute lounge. He almost filled the small room as he stood waiting for her and she summoned up all her courage to look him full in the face, her senses registering a whiff of the familiar aftershave at the same time as her toes curled at the sheer attractiveness of the man. He did look so…good, she thought desperately as she took in the rugged, hard face, and she didn't want to think like this, she didn't want to at all. The man was probably here to demand all manner of retribution.

''I'm here to say you were right—partly,'' he said immediately her eyes met his, ''and I'm prepared to admit there were some mistakes made with the way Steel Enterprises took hold of your father's business.''

''Oh.'' It was the last thing she had expected and it took all lucid thought from her mind.

''That doesn't excuse your disgraceful behaviour on Friday evening,'' he continued tightly, ''the repercussions of which I shall have to deal with for a long, long time.''

''Well, excuse me,'' she said with hot sarcasm, ''but you'll understand if that little detail doesn't bother me too much in view of the fact that you are at least around to deal with them, unlike my father.'' She glared at him angrily.

"You understand it was perfectly legal?" he asked coldly as he held her glance. "Within the law?"

"Legal?" She repeated the word as though it was repugnant to her. "And that makes everything all right, I suppose?"

"Of course not," he said sharply. "I was merely making the point for future reference."

"Well, bully for you." She sat down on the settee as her legs began to shake. "But you aren't at a board meeting now. Can't you talk in normal language?"

He stared at her for a long moment and then let the breath out through his teeth in a slow hiss. "I'm nervous," he said with devastating honesty. "This is new territory—I'm not used to admitting we've got it wrong."

"Now that I can believe," she said with less acerbity than she would have liked. The almost fierce truthfulness was totally disarming. But maybe that was what he was hoping to achieve? He was a multi-millionaire used to manipulating hundreds of people to his will. What chance did she stand against a mind like that? About the same as her father, she would think.

"You're not going to give an inch, are you?" He lifted her chin suddenly, his hand firm, looking deep into her eyes as he shook his head slowly. "Your eyes are big and dark and full of a wary kind of hate," he said quietly. "I thought women were supposed to be the weaker sex?"

Her mouth was dry and she found she couldn't get the words she wanted to say past her parched lips. She wet them with her tongue, aware that the razor-sharp gaze followed the gesture as his eyes narrowed.

"What are you going to do?" she asked defiantly as she jerked herself free from his hold. "I know you're furious with me, the papers were every bit as bad as you had guessed, so what's the next step?" She took a step backwards as she spoke, feeling a little safer as the space increased between them. "I'd rather know now, if you don't mind. I don't like the cat-and-mouse games you seem to enjoy."

"Is that a fact?" The words were abrupt and fierce and then he seemed to take an almost conscious hold on his temper, straightening his features as he looked at her again. "The thing is, from my investigations so far it's clear mistakes were made, of a moral nature, you understand?"

"Oh, I understand all right," she said flatly.

"For the record, it is not the normal way we conduct negotiations, but someone was rather too enthusiastic."

"Too enthusiastic?" she repeated icily. "Well, if you call using some heavy pressure to get banks to refuse loan extensions and causing contracts to die mid-stream 'enthusiasm', you're in a worse state of moral decline than I thought. Your company ran my father out of business, within the *law*, of course," she added sarcastically, "and picked up the premises for a song. The Mafia couldn't have handled it better."

"A slight exaggeration," he said tightly.

"Do you know who was in charge of it all?" she asked suddenly.

"Possibly," he said with a vague wave of his hand.

"Possibly." She looked at him angrily. "And what are you going to do about it?"

"I think you can leave that with me." The blue eyes flicked over her hot face. "Would you like to discuss your fate over dinner?" he asked expressionlessly, his eyes hooded.

"What?" She stared at him in total amazement. "Me have dinner with you?"

"What is so outrageous about that?" he asked softly.

"Mr Steel, I wouldn't have dinner with you again if you were the last man on earth," she said flatly. "I'm not at all sure you weren't spear-heading this thing for a start and, even if you weren't, I don't believe you wouldn't have had some knowledge of it at the time. You can tell me my fate now."

"Are you calling me a liar?" The deep voice was even softer now, but with a coldness that chilled her blood.

"I think that's exactly what I was saying, yes." Her voice was cutting. "I appreciate your coming here—"

"Well, that's a start at least." He reached her side in one stride and stood looking down at her, his height accentuated even more by the bulky dark overcoat he was wearing. "What do I have to do to get that closed little mind to open just the merest crack?" The azure eyes wandered over her face lazily and she took a deep silent breath as the subtle magnetism that was an integral part of his make-up reached out to her. His face was disturbing, a cynical sensuality carved into its

harsh lines that was savagely attractive, but there was
more to his appeal than mere looks. It was everything
about him, she thought weakly: the intimidating self-
control, the fierce authority that was in every glance,
every action, and went hand in hand with total domination. He was walking dynamite and she knew nothing at all about explosives.

"Why bother, Mr Steel?" she asked with as much
acidity as she could muster. "I'm just your average
working girl; there's nothing special about me."

"Wrong." The cool arrogance was incredibly infuriating.

She shrugged as casually as she could, considering
he was far too close for comfort. "Most people would
disagree with you," she said shortly.

"Then most people are fools." His expression was
impossible to fathom and she stared at him for a moment, silently trying to gauge the hidden thoughts in
that cold, analytical mind. This was a trap of some
kind, but she couldn't work out what.

During a lunchtime sandwich taken at her office
desk she had asked Joe, very nonchalantly, just what
sort of a man he thought Kane Steel was and she remembered the sharp, piercing look of concern that had
straightened Joe's blunt features. "Not your sort," he
had replied immediately, "although it would surprise
me if he had been in on the little deal you mentioned.
That's not his usual way of doing things. He's very
tough, very ruthless, quite without a shred of self-
doubt or remorse, but he's straight—or I thought he
was." Her employer's eyes had been narrowed with

alarm. "Don't get interested in him, Janie; he's totally out of your league. Apart from his wealth and power, the man has a big appetite, know what I mean?"

"You mean women?" she'd asked quietly.

"Definitely the plural," Joe had said drily. "And they love him. I've yet to see him with the same one twice."

"Oh." She had glanced down at the papers on her desk as she put the suddenly tasteless sandwich back on the plate. "I just wondered."

"Quit wondering." Joe's voice had been a hard warning.

The conversation had cut deep and now, as she looked up at the chiselled features, she wondered why. She didn't know him, she didn't want to know him. It didn't matter to her if he had five or fifty women in tow!

"Well, I appreciate your coming, Mr Steel—" she began again, only to come to an abrupt halt as he put a firm finger over her lips.

"You've already said that." His deep voice was like silk. "You realise, of course, that we've got rather a lot to discuss? Besides your penance, that is."

"Not that I'm aware of." She stared at him militantly as she took a step or two backwards. "I really can't think of a thing."

"Well, for a start there's the amount your father's firm was acquired for." He was watching her intently. "Are you familiar with the figures?"

"Not really," she admitted slowly. "I've got the papers somewhere, of course, but I haven't looked through them since he died. I just noticed then it was a give-away, but I think he'd got to the point where he was grateful he wasn't going to have to declare bankruptcy. Things got pretty nasty for a while.'' Her eyes were bright with accusation.

''I've got people working on a more realistic figure,'' he said quietly, ''and of course, as his daughter, you would receive the payment.''

''I don't want your money!'' As the full realisation of where the conversation was heading dawned on her, Janie flushed scarlet, her eyes horrified as they met his cool blue gaze. ''This isn't about money—is that what you thought? I wanted to tell you exactly what I thought of you, that was all. I wouldn't take a penny of your money.''

''If it's a fair price for the property it's hardly my money, is it?'' he said reasonably. ''We're talking about what your father was due—''

''But you can't give *him* what he was due,'' she said hotly. ''It's too late for that. I don't want money. I want my father alive and well; but that's impossible.''

''I know this is an emotional subject but can't you be a little more reasonable?'' he asked tightly as she glared up at him, her eyes flashing. ''It was *you* who lampooned *me*, remember!''

''That was nothing to what I'd have liked to have done and I don't want blood money, can't you get that through your head? You can't buy off a guilty conscience like that. You'll have to live with what you did,'' she said bitterly.

"For crying out loud!" He put his hand to his head as he swung round angrily and walked across to the tiny window that overlooked the dark street below. "*I* didn't do anything; I've told you."

"So you have." She didn't know quite what was driving her to act like this, but she knew it was more than the old hurt and pain for her father. Beyond that her brain refused to think. "I'd like you to leave now, Mr Steel."

"Certainly." He swung round, but in doing so stumbled slightly as though the movement had caught him off balance and, again, her senses registered that unsteadiness in his bearing that was recovered instantly as he strode across the room, his face black with rage. "You are a very exasperating young woman, Miss Janie Gordon," he said tightly as he moved into the tiny hall.

"I won't tell you what I think of you," she returned derisively, her face full of burning contempt. "But it's not good."

For an instant his eyes slid over the dark, silky shoulder-length hair, angry red mouth and burning velvet-brown eyes, and his gaze narrowed forebodingly. "You don't have to," he said mockingly, "and, as you consider me to be the lowest of the low, I'll just play true to type."

As he caught hold of her slender wrists, imprisoning them securely in one large brown hand, she felt the leashed strength that the big body had under perfect control, and realised that he hadn't lost his temper, that this was a cold-blooded exercise in punishment of her defiance. She made a token effort of resistance but, having felt the hard power of his arms before, knew it was useless even as she twisted in his grasp. ''You are your own worst enemy; has anyone else ever told you that?'' he asked softly as his mouth descended on hers in bruising exploration.

Even as her body filled with outrage at the liberty he was taking, another, more insidious, frightening emotion took its place. His touch was so sensual, so fascinating that even as she fought to retain her defences they were all swept away. He's just too good at this, she thought despairingly. He didn't use one iota more force than he had to in order to subdue her, his lips possessive and erotic rather than violent, but as an electrifying explosion of warmth seared along her limbs she realised he had anticipated her response. He was a man who understood women, she thought blindly, knew how to mould them to his will.

His free hand had moved her body into his, his arm vice-like round the small of her back, and the sheer power in the big male frame fitted against her softness caused her to shudder with excitement and fear. How did she fight him, she asked herself desperately, when all her body and mind was engaged in the struggle not to succumb completely to the trembling pleasure that was flooding every nerve-end, every cell of her body with flickering warmth?

The kiss could only have lasted for minutes, but when he released her she felt strange, almost drugged, and it was a second or two before she pulled herself together sufficiently to move away. "I hate you." Her voice was thick and shaky.

"Maybe." As she raised her eyes to his face she expected mockery, perhaps even contempt at his easy mastery of her defences, but the hard, attractive face was inscrutable, betraying nothing. "Maybe not."

"I do." The relief of tears was a luxury she couldn't indulge in, not now, not in front of him, and she bit her lip so hard, she felt the taste of blood in her mouth. "I never want to see you again in my life."

"I can't promise that," he said softly as he opened the front door with cold arrogance. "You'll just have to live in hope, won't you?"

As the door shut behind him, she leapt across the hall and shot the bolt loudly into place, her hands trembling. He was despicable, worse even than she had thought, a cold-hearted bully without a trace of normal human warmth... She found herself pacing the flat blindly and put her hands to her hot face as she sank down on to the worn carpet with a little shuddering cry. She hated him; she really did. He was everything she despised in a man...

The next few days brought their own kind of comfort in their very routine and normality and, as the week drew to a close, she began to breathe more easily. He wouldn't try and make contact again, she reassured herself for the umpteenth time as she sat writing Christmas cards in the warm glow from her little gas fire while the wind hurled sleet at the window on an icy, wintry Sunday afternoon. It was all over, finished, a difficult and humiliating episode in her life which, with hindsight, she had handled with more fury than wisdom, but it had been something she had had to see through. She nodded as she sealed the last of the white square envelopes. So why was she feeling so…odd?

She paced restlessly into the tiny kitchen and made herself a mug of strong black coffee. She wouldn't allow herself to become maudlin, not for a minute! She wandered back into the lounge and switched on her small portable TV set aimlessly. Immediately, the tiny room was filled with the strains of "Silent Night' as a circle of bright-eyed children stared back at her from the flickering screen.

Two weeks to Christmas. She glanced at the pile of cards thoughtfully. Since her father had died she had spent the last two Christmases with her aunt's family—her mother's sister—arriving on Christmas Eve and staying until Boxing Day afternoon, and had thoroughly enjoyed the break with her aunt and uncle and cousins. They had invited her again this year and she was looking forward to it—one of her cousins had just had twins and she couldn't wait to see the two tiny boys. And on her return here she had several party invitations and numerous requests to join friends for "drinks". She was most fortunate. She nodded again sharply. She *was*. And right from this minute she was going to put all thoughts of a certain man totally and completely out of her mind and get on with her life.

The flu bug hit the office the next week and within days the workforce was halved. "Just before

Christmas,'' Joe muttered desperately on the Friday afternoon as he arrived back from a photo session that had gone painfully wrong only to find yet another of his staff gone. ''I don't suppose you could work this weekend, Janie?'' he added hopefully as he looked round the empty desks in the main office.

''Consider it done,'' she said cheerfully, feeling slightly guilty at Joe's effusive thanks. To be honest, the empty flat had oppressed her the last few days and she couldn't think why. The extra work would keep her mind occupied and, besides, she loved her job; working with Joe was always interesting and often hilarious and he was a good friend besides being her boss.

By the following Friday she had worked twelve days from eight in the morning until nine at night without a break and was feeling the strain. The pace was even more hectic than usual and, although some of the original staff were back, others had taken their places on the sick list. On Saturday there was a major panic that necessitated her staying in the office until almost midnight and returning at seven the next morning and when she awoke on the Monday with heavy aching eyes and a dull throb at the back of her head she put it down to near exhaustion, crawling into work on trembling legs with tender muscles she never knew she had.

Wednesday, Christmas Eve, took on the appearance of an oasis in the desert and, although she tried to convince herself that another forty-eight hours were not beyond her, by mid-afternoon on Monday she had admitted to herself that the symptoms were flu and was on her way home in the back of Joe's Italian sports car feeling like death.

"Are you going to be all right?" Joe stood in her tiny hall, obviously itching to get back to the chaos in his office, and she waved him away with a firm nod.

"I shall take some aspirin and go to bed," she said weakly.

"Well, stay there until you feel better," he said as he backed towards the door. "I shan't expect to see you again until after Christmas. Your Christmas box is in the card." He placed a large envelope on the hall table and was gone.

She felt worse the next day, crawling out of bed for the odd hot drink and aspirin and then falling back into the welcoming warmth with dizzy thankfulness.

Christmas Eve dawned to the sound of icy rain beating a tattoo against the window and the knowledge that there was no way she could inflict herself on her aunt's household, especially with two new-born babies in residence. She phoned her aunt once the rest of the world was awake and then spent most of the day in a semi-doze, feeling tremendously sorry for herself whenever she surfaced out of the thick stupor.

"What a Christmas," she muttered to herself in the late evening when her aching back drove her from her bed into an armchair in front of the fire where she sat cocooned in a huge patchwork quilt with a large box of tissues and a cheese sandwich that she couldn't bring herself to eat.

When the doorbell rang it seemed like the final

straw. She ignored it twice but on the third vicious jab it became apparent that whoever was outside could hear her TV and didn't intend to go away. "Damn, damn, damn…" She staggered to her feet with the quilt still wrapped round her and a tissue in each hand, catching sight of herself in the thin full-length mirror in the hall just before she opened the door. What a mess! Tangled hair, white face, red nose—not exactly the spirit of Christmas, she thought, with a wry grimace at the pale reflection that stared back at her with pink-rimmed eyes. Unless it was a caricature of one of Santa's gnomes. And she felt so light-headed, so dizzy.

"I've had some papers drawn up." As the door swung open that familiar deep voice sounded somewhere over her head at the same time as her stunned mind registered an enormous figure in a dark overcoat, complete with briefcase, standing in the opening. "Janie…?"

No power on earth could have prevented her from falling into the rushing blackness that was enveloping every part of her body, and as she sank helplessly to the floor she was aware, with a tiny detached part of her brain that still seemed to be functioning normally, that Kane Steel's face was a picture of horrified panic and alarm, and she knew a moment of deep and gratifying satisfaction that for once she had caught him completely at a loss.

# CHAPTER FOUR

JANIE came to on a wave of exhausted weakness, to find herself immersed in the depths of the patchwork quilt, propped cocoon-fashion in the armchair, with Kane Steel's dark face an inch from her own.

"Everything's all right. Don't be frightened." It came to her, as his deep rich voice spoke softly in her ear, that he was the only person on earth she had any reason *to* fear and the thought brought a bubble of almost hysterical amusement to the surface as she struggled to take a grip on herself. "How do you feel?" he asked gently as she continued to stare dazedly into his face.

"Like death warmed up," she whispered honestly. A burst of laughter from the TV broke jarringly into the room and he indicated the television with a sharp wave of his hand.

"Can I turn it off?"

"Yes, do." She watched him as he moved to flick the small switch, noticing the dark hair gleaming with life and the tiny drops of water from the unremitting sleet outside, the big, capable body and attractive, harsh face. His vitality and strength filled the small room with energy and vivid force, and she felt a moment's breathless panic at her own frailty. She felt vulnerable and weak and miserable, and she needed to be strong in front of this man, always. He would capitalise on any feebleness, going straight for the jugular, she *knew* it. Compassion was something alien to him. Look at all Joe had told her, what he had done to her father, everything...

He broke into her racing feverish thoughts by turning back to her and taking her small hand in his. "How long have you been like this?" he asked softly.

She had forgotten the riveting blueness of his eyes, she thought irrelevantly as she tried to force a reply from the cotton wool in her head. They must be the most stunningly beautiful eyes she had ever seen: ice-blue and almost depthless.

"Janie?" He squeezed her hand gently. "How long have you been ill?"

"Since Monday." She forced the thickness from her brain with tremendous effort. "It's only the flu. Everyone's had it at work."

"I see." He rose and stood looking down at her for a moment before walking through to the tiny kitchen. "Do you want tea or coffee?" he called blandly.

"There's no need—" She stopped abruptly as he reappeared in the doorway, dark eyebrows raised sternly over determined eyes. "Tea, please," she finished weakly.

"Have you had the doctor?" He had returned with two mugs of steaming tea in an incredibly short time and as she sipped the hot liquid gratefully she felt tears pricking at the backs of her eyes for no reason at all that she could think of. It was annoying to feel so weak when she needed to be strong.

"Of course not." She pushed back her mop of tangled black curls with a shaky hand. "I told you, it's just the flu."

"There's no such thing as 'just the flu'," he said sharply. "It can be the very devil, in all sorts of ways. Does your chest hurt? Earache?"

"Oh, for goodness' sake..." She eyed him balefully. "Do you make this much fuss when you're ill? A few days and I'll be as right as rain. I feel better already, actually," she lied unconvincingly.

"Well, you look dreadful," he said flatly.

"Charming." A deeper stain of red joined the feverish flush on her cheekbones. "That's just what I needed to hear."

"Who's looking after you?" His glance moved round the tiny room as though he expected someone to materialise out of the woodwork. "Your fridge is all but empty—that's the last drop of milk in the tea."

"I'm looking after me," she said, "and you can go now. I really can't look at any papers now," she added as she caught sight of his briefcase against the coffee-table. "Are they hostile or friendly?"

"You mean there isn't anyone looking in on you, doing the errands and so on?" he asked, ignoring the latter part of her words with regal indifference. "Are you spending Christmas with anyone—relatives?"

"I was going to." She fiddled with the edge of the quilt without looking at him. "But then I got flu and my cousin has just had twin boys; I couldn't risk them catching this.''

"I see.'' He stood up slowly. "So in effect you are all alone with hardly any food in the house and it's six o'clock on Christmas Eve. Who did you expect to feed you for the next couple of days—Santa Claus?''

"There's no need for sarcasm,'' she said tightly as the anger he always seemed to ignite surged through her system. "I don't feel like eating anyway.''

He shook his head slowly as he stood looking down at her, an expression in his eyes that she couldn't quite fathom. "I don't think I've ever met anyone quite like you in my life,'' he said quietly. "Were you born this difficult and independent, or did you take lessons?''

"Look, I didn't ask you to come here tonight,'' she said tensely, "and how I run my life is up to me and me alone. I wouldn't exactly say you're in a position to criticise other people's shortcomings, certainly not from where I'm standing.''

"Sitting.'' He seemed quite unmoved by her outburst.

"What?'' She stared at him in confusion.

"You're sitting, not standing,'' he said shortly, "and there is no way I'm walking out of here and leaving you alone in the state you're in.''

"I'm not in a state,'' she objected indignantly, "or I wasn't until you came.'' It was blatantly untrue but just at that moment she didn't care. "I shall be perfectly all right. I'm warm, I've got the TV—''

"And no food, no company.'' He eyed her impassively. "This will certainly be a Christmas to remember, won't it?"

She shut her eyes for a moment as a wave of dizziness swept over her. It was having to look up at him, she thought irritably. He really was the most arrogantly maddening man she had ever met in her life. And the most attractive. Her eyes opened wide as the thought popped unbidden into her mind and she stared at him for a moment, horror-stricken. "Look, just go, will you?" she said weakly.

"Sorry." He smiled imperturbably. "I can't do that. Now, where's your toothbrush?"

"My toothbrush?" She was hallucinating now, she thought desperately, but it had sounded for all the world as though he had asked where her toothbrush was.

"Yes, your toothbrush," he said with enormous and obvious patience. "In fact, all your toiletries, and you'd better bring a change of nightclothes, too. I suppose there's a suitcase in the bedroom somewhere?"

As he glanced round for the appropriate door she let out a squeak of pure panic. "Now just hang on a moment. What on earth do you think you're suggesting?" she asked faintly.

"I'm not 'suggesting' anything, Janie," he said drily, his eyes fastening back on hers with that disturbing intentness that was quite unnerving. "I'm taking you home with me, of course."

"You're not, you know," she said sharply, with a flash of her old fighting spirit. "I've got flu, not brain damage! I'm not going anywhere with you."

"I seem to remember we've had this conversation before," he drawled expressionlessly as he pointed towards one of the doors leading off the tiny lounge. "Is that the bedroom?"

"Will you *listen*?" She rose, with extreme difficulty considering that the quilt was wrapped round her body like swaddling clothes, and moved to stand in front of him, her small face lifted up to the sardonic darkness of his. "I can manage perfectly well here and I've got no intention of going to your house again, especially at Christmas when all your arrangements must be made. If you want to do anything at all, a quick visit to the corner shop would suffice for some milk and stuff. OK?"

"I've listened." The faintly bored expression hadn't altered at all. "Now, where's the suitcase—or maybe you're happy to come just as you are? And sit down. I've already picked you up off the floor once and you were a dead weight," he finished ungallantly.

"Oh, you—you—"

"I know, I know." He smiled mockingly. "You loathe and detest the very ground I walk on—we'll take that as read—but nevertheless you are leaving here with me in the next sixty seconds—with or without your permission."

"It'll be without," she snapped furiously and he nodded slowly, his eyes glittering blue fire.

"Fine." He had whisked her up into his arms before she had time to protest and for a moment the stunned surprise, combined with her muzzy head, made any speech impossible. "Are your keys in your handbag?"

He flicked the bag off a side-table with one finger as he walked with her to the door.

"Yes, but—"

"No more buts." He looked down at her seriously and suddenly she was aware that her heart was thumping violently—and not with anger—as she became aware of the all-enveloping power of the man. The strong, capable arms that held her so securely were draining her will to resist. It felt good to be looked after, cared for, and as she closed her eyes and let her head sink against the hard male chest she missed the tightening of his sensual mouth when he glanced down at her bent head. It was ridiculous, crazy, and she was going to regret it bitterly when sanity reasserted itself, she thought weakly, but just now the temptation to let him take control was too strong to resist. She felt tired and ill and confused, and the thought of being able to lean on someone else, albeit for just a short while, was seductively good.

He didn't say a word until he had installed her in the back of the Bentley although she caught the incredulous face of Baines in the front seat for a fleeting moment before Kane placed her, very gently, into the car's warm interior. "I shall need the keys to turn off the lights," he said quietly as he placed her handbag on her lap. "Is there a neighbour you want me to leave a message with, to reassure them I'm not a white-slave trader or something?"

"They're all away." She spoke before she had time to think and he shook his head slowly as his eyes wandered over her face.

"And you were going to be there all alone over the Christmas period?" he said condemningly.

"Well, I didn't plan to be," she said quickly. "I told you, the twins and everything." She squared her shoulders under the heavy quilt. "Anyway, I can look after myself."

"It seemed like it when I picked you up off the carpet." He took the keys from her hand with a little nod and turned away, shutting the door behind him.

"Kane!" She banged on the window to attract his attention and he opened the door again. "My toothbrush and things are on the windowsill in the bathroom," she said in a very small voice, "and there are some other clothes and a suitcase in the wardrobe in the bedroom."

"Right." His voice was bland but the dark face expressed satisfaction at her capitulation. "Can we keep it at that now?" he asked mildly as he remained looking into the car's interior.

"What?" She stared at him bewilderedly.

"Kane." He eyed her wickedly. "We aren't going to digress back to Mr Steel when you're *compos mentis*, are we?"

She held his glance for a long moment before allowing a small smile to touch the edge of her mouth. "No," she admitted reluctantly. "It's Kane now."

"And here was I thinking I was too old to write to Father Christmas," he drawled mockingly, "but the old man came through after all." He had shut the car door again before she could reply, which was just as well as there was something in his face she didn't care to define.

She jumped violently as Baines drew back the glass partition a second later, and the middle-aged man nodded apologetically in her direction. "Sorry, miss, didn't mean to make you jump. You're not well, then?"

"Flu." She gave a wan smile. "I've been fine all year and then, just at Christmas…"

"Always the way, miss, always the way." He glanced at her white face consideringly. "I'd lie back and close your eyes now, miss; you look all in." She did as he suggested, listening to the harsh driving rain lashing against the car windows as she snuggled deeper into the warm quilt, her tired mind going into a suspended animation where only the physical senses were real: warmth, comfort and total relaxation.

She must have actually slept in the few minutes before Kane returned with her old battered suitcase because she woke with a strange sense of disorientation as he clambered back into the car, icy particles of rain clinging to his coat and hair.

"What a night!" He settled down beside her and nodded at Baines to drive off. "And look what the wind's blown in." There was something deep and soft in his voice as his piercing eyes stroked their blueness over her face while she sat looking at him quietly.

"This is very kind of you," she said after a full minute had elapsed and her cheeks were glowing with colour.

"You think so?" he asked softly. "It's not really.

I could hardly leave you in such a condition and go back to eat a hearty Christmas dinner, could I? Could I?'' The rugged, attractive face broke into a smile that stopped her heart beating for a split-second, only for it to roar away like an express train. Was this the face he showed his women? her mind asked her a moment later when her pounding heart was under control again. If so, she didn't doubt the truth of Joe's words—they *would* love him. The combination of fierce masculinity and tender warmth was frighteningly seductive, but she knew the other side. She shut her eyes as her mind ground relentlessly on. Her father had experienced at first hand the particular brand of ruthless callousness this man was so good at, whether directly from himself or one of his minions who no doubt had been encouraged to think they were acting as the great man himself would.

*She mustn't forget the past.* The thought hammered in her mind as the big car ate up the miles with effortless ease. All this care and attention spoke heavily of a guilty conscience which was an indictment in itself, and if she forgot all that she'd been told and, more importantly, what she *knew* the consequences would be fair and squarely on her own head. And yet was he really as heartless as she had supposed? For the last two years the very thought of this man had been enough to make her flesh creep, but now? She glanced at him from under her thick, silky lashes. If her flesh crept now it was for quite a different reason. And that just wasn't good enough. She should never have let him persuade her to come with him, she thought, suddenly panic-stricken. She was playing with fire.

"You're frowning again."

"What?" As her eyes snapped to meet his she saw his dark face was full of mockery.

"You were thinking of me then, weren't you?" he said drily. "Stirring up the fires of rage and recrimination? Can't you just lie back and be ill and let me take the load? I am offering you the hospitality of my home for a couple of days until you can stand on your own two feet again, that's all, I promise. I'd do the same for anyone."

"Would you?" she asked doubtfully and then flushed violently as he burst into a bellow of delighted laughter.

"You're priceless, do you know that? You have the most expressive face of any female I know. Are you always this candid?"

"Yes." She faced him squarely now, her brown eyes huge in the dim light. "Always. My father was a great one for honesty whether in business or private. He used to say that, although it might cost sometimes, in the long run to be any different took a greater price from the essence of one's spirit." His face straightened at the bitterness that flooded into her eyes. "But you wouldn't understand that, of course."

"Of course." His voice was splinter-sharp.

She had expected him to defend himself, to reiterate his innocence, but as the blue eyes fastened on her face, their arctic colour as hard as stone, he settled back in his seat with a deep sigh. "Relax, Janie," he said flatly as his features settled into an expressionless mask. "I know exactly what you think of me and I like my women to be receptive, if not willing. You are perfectly safe."

They didn't speak again until the big car nosed its way to the bottom of the wide stone steps leading up to the huge front door and by then Janie felt too ill to object when Kane reached into the car and lifted her out into his arms. Her head was pounding and she felt incredibly tired. The brief spell of activity had exhausted her more than she would have thought possible. "I'm going to take you straight upstairs and Mrs Langton will take care of you," he said quietly as Baines opened the front door just in front of them. "OK?"

She nodded wearily and then gasped with wonder as Kane stepped into the warmth of the house. A huge Christmas tree, its green branches heavily laden with tinsel, glass baubles and tiny, beautifully wrapped parcels in varying shades of red and gold dominated the vast hall, the sweet smell of pine redolent in the warm air. "Is it real?" He was halfway across the hall when she spoke and he paused to look down at her, his dark face expressionless.

"Oh, yes, quite real," he said softly. "Do you approve?"

"It's beautiful." For the first time the reality that it really *was* Christmas washed over her. The frantic pace at the office for the last two weeks, combined with the attack of flu, had taken the serene magic she normally felt at the birth of the Christ child out of her mind. "Absolutely beautiful." She raised her eyes to his face and saw the stern mouth was smiling slightly at her undisguised delight.

"We tend to go over the top at Christmas," he said with no apparent sign of remorse, "but then it is a special time of the year, isn't it?" The blue eyes softened as he held her gaze. "A time of rejoicing, of happiness, of...forgiveness?" The last word was a question she was incapable of answering and as she stared at him mutely she began to feel as though she would drown in the blue of his eyes. His face was close, so close, and the delicious aftershave he wore reached out to pull her even closer. "Happy Christmas, Janie." As he lightly brushed her lips with his own she felt their contact as though they burnt and the jerk of her head was more shock than withdrawal, but violent nevertheless.

His mouth tightened at the gesture, but in the next instant Mrs Langton and June had arrived on the scene, their exclamations of concern demanding explanation as Kane carried her towards the stairs.

"Are the guest bedrooms made up, Mrs Langton?" he asked over his shoulder as he began to climb the massive staircase.

"Yes, sir, with two spare," the housekeeper replied behind him. "I would suggest you put Miss Gordon in the mauve suite. Facing the gardens as it does, it's a little quieter than some of the others."

"Yes, that would be ideal." They reached one huge landing that wound away into the distance in a mass of ankle-deep carpeting and cream-linen walls, and then they were climbing more stairs. On the next floor Kane turned sharply to the right and waited as Mrs Langton opened a beautifully carved oak door in front of him to reveal a sumptuously luxurious sitting-room, tastefully decorated in shades of mauve and complete with a huge TV, soft upholstered armchairs and occasional tables. He carried her straight through this first room and into one beyond which boasted two full-size double beds, what looked like a walk-in wardrobe all down one wall, heavy velvet drapes which Mrs Langton quickly pulled against the driving rain outside and a general feeling of comfort and luxury that was quite beyond Janie's normal comprehension.

"Mrs Langton will settle you in and then we'll see about a meal," Kane said shortly as he placed her carefully into a large cane chair while the housekeeper and little maid quickly pulled back the covers of the nearest bed, switching on the electric blanket as they did so, and then helped her out of the swaths of the patchwork quilt once Kane had left the room.

"What a shame, miss, on Christmas Eve 'n' all," the little maid said chattily as Janie slid thankfully under the covers. A definite sense of unreality had her head spinning as the sudden change in her circumstances overwhelmed her. The vast room was the last word in comfort and she felt dazed at the thought that such rich opulence was perfectly ordinary to him— commonplace.

Why had she ever approached him that fateful evening? she thought numbly as great waves of tiredness swept over her in a consuming flood. Why hadn't she been content to hate him from afar? It would have been better, so much better... She was unaware that she had fallen asleep even as Mrs Langton asked her about a meal, unaware of the two women slipping quietly out of the room and shutting the door gently behind them, unaware of anything at all...

"Miss Gordon?" She rose from thick layers of sleep with her limbs feeling like lead and a muzzy sensation in her head which clouded thought. "You really must try and eat something and then we'll leave you in peace." Mrs Langton and June were standing at the side of the bed, the little maid holding a tray on which a steaming bowl of soup and two bread rolls reposed, along with a small glass of fresh orange juice.

"What time is it?" Janie struggled into a sitting position and glanced about her dazedly, her head thudding.

"Nine o'clock," the housekeeper replied quietly. "You've been asleep for an hour or so, but Mr Steel wants you to try and have some nourishment before you settle down for the night."

She had never felt less like food in her life, but under the eagle eyes of Mrs Langton she managed to force down a few mouthfuls of soup and half a bread roll, and finish the glass of orange juice. "Good girl." As Mrs Langton whisked the tray away and helped her ease back down under the covers Janie felt like a small child again; the housekeeper really was most formidable.

Kane entered the room as the tall, severe woman

left and immediately Janie's nerves went into over-drive. He had changed into casual clothes and looked incredibly tall and attractive in a thick Aran jumper and light cream trousers that made his dark skin even more bronzed. She felt sticky and crumpled and strangely crushed, and it didn't help to see him fairly brimming with health and vitality.

"You managed a little food?" he said approvingly. "I thought if I sent Mrs Langton in for the first assault it might work. There aren't many people who can refuse her when she's at her most determined."

"I can imagine," Janie agreed weakly.

"She's got a heart of gold, though," he continued quietly as he moved the chair closer to the bed and sat down, crossing one muscled leg over the other. "Brought up six children single-handed when her husband died, leaving her a widow at the age of thirty-two, and all of them doing well for themselves."

"Oh." His closeness was giving her body's heating system cause for concern; from being shivery and shaky she now felt warm all over to the point where she was sure her cheeks and nose were glowing an unattractive shade of red.

"You look very small and very vulnerable in there," he said suddenly as his eyes stroked over her hot face consideringly, "and very beautiful."

"Beautiful?" Her face expressed her disbelief. "I look a mess."

"A beautiful mess." His voice was deep and soft and seductively warm, and a little shiver started at the top of her spine and worked its way down to her toes.

"Who would have thought I'd be spending Christmas Eve sitting in a chair at the side of your bed?" he added wickedly as the glow spread up into her hair.

"Who indeed?" she said sarcastically as she tried to pull herself together. "I suppose *in* it would be more in your usual line of things."

"Do you indeed?" He settled back in the chair and surveyed her through cool, narrowed eyes. "Been hearing stories about the big bad wolf?" His smile didn't reach his eyes. "What have you got me down as—a ravager of maidens and a despoiler of virgins?"

"Don't be ridiculous." The conversation was fast getting out of control and she searched for a way to end it. "There's no need for you to stay here anyway. I don't want to spoil your Christmas," she added weakly.

"I like being here." He reached across and touched her burning cheeks with a cool hand. "But I'm not at all sure I shouldn't call the doctor."

"Don't you dare!" She flicked away his hand irritably. "This only normally lasts forty-eight hours, but I was a bit tired before it hit me. I shall be as right as rain tomorrow."

"I doubt it." He reached across to the small bookcase in an alcove by the bed and selected a novel before seating himself again. "Go to sleep like a good girl, then," he said comfortably as he opened the book.

"I can't sleep with you sitting there," she said in amazement as her stomach contracted at the thought.

"Why not?" He eyed her through half-closed lids.

"Because it's not—I can't—" She stumbled to an abrupt halt. "I just can't, that's all," she finished sharply.

"Don't be such a prude," he said smoothly as his gaze fixed fully on her face again. "What do you think I'm going to do—leap on you as soon as you're asleep?"

"Of course not." She wouldn't have thought it was possible for her face to get any hotter, but it did. "I just don't think it's necessary, that's all."

"Well, I do," he said imperturbably. "You've fainted once, you're very hot and feverish and I shan't leave here until I'm satisfied you're all right. Now, go to sleep."

"Are you always this pigheaded?" she asked crossly as he glanced down at the book again.

"Always." He didn't raise his head as he spoke and she lay looking at him for a moment, uncertain of what to say next. The thick black hair was truly black, she thought inconsequentially as she noticed a faintly blue gleam to the shining strands in the artificial light. That was unusual when taken with the cool, ice-blue eyes.

"Are your parents Irish?" she asked suddenly as the thought popped into her mind.

"My parents?" She had surprised him, she thought gleefully as he raised startled eyes to her face. "I don't understand."

"Your colouring," she explained quickly. "It's uncommon to find such dark hair and blue eyes."

"My mother's Irish," he said after a long moment.

"Blame it on her. My father is as English as they come."

"They're still alive?" she asked curiously.

"Alive and kicking." That breathtakingly sweet smile she had seen once before made a brief appearance. "They live in France now, though. My father suffers from arthritis and finds the mild climate of Provence more to his liking." She nodded slowly. "You'll probably meet them tomorrow," he finished surprisingly. "They're staying with me for a few days."

"You didn't inherit all this, then?" If she had been fully awake she probably wouldn't have asked such impertinent questions, but the dozy warmth that she had slid into, combined with the unreality of the situation, seemed to have put them on a different plane.

"Partly." He seemed quite unperturbed by her curiosity. "My maternal grandparents were very rich and left everything to be divided equally between my brother and myself. About the same time they died I discovered I had a flair for wheeling and dealing despite a very adequate university education which I chose to ignore. The rest, as they say, is history."

She nodded again. Her eyelids were really very heavy—she'd just shut them for a few moments. As she did so he rose and turned off the main light, switching a small bedside light on a moment later and turning it round to shine fully on his seat.

"Goodnight, Janie." She felt his lips brush hers, their texture firm and warm, but pretended she was asleep as her heart thudded into her throat, and there was a long moment of silence before she heard him settle himself back in the seat. And then she slept.

# CHAPTER FIVE

WHEN Janie awoke the next morning it was to an empty room and the knowledge that she felt immeasurably better. She lay for a moment in the warmth of the big bed as she stretched carefully, relieved to find that the grinding aches and pains that had racked her body for the last few days were just an unpleasant memory.

The polite knock at the door and June's entrance were simultaneous, and as the young maid saw her struggling to sit up in the fleecy depths of the bed she smiled cheerfully, her bright face aglow. "You're awake, then, miss," she said heartily as she placed a cup of tea on the bedside cabinet and walked across to pull the heavy curtains. "Mr Steel said the fever had broken last night when he left your room and that you were sleeping like a baby. My mum always says that sleep's the best medicine she knows."

"Does she?" Janie smiled as the young girl walked back to stand at the side of the bed. "I'd have thought you would have gone home for Christmas, but perhaps Mr Steel couldn't spare you?"

"Oh, no, miss; he said I could have the week off if I wanted," June said quickly, "but there's ten of us at home in a three-bedroomed flat and it's murder. I'd much rather be here. I have to share a bedroom with my three little sisters at home, and you know what kids are. Here, I've got my own room and TV and bathroom—I love it." She smiled guiltily. "That sounds awful, doesn't it? I do love my mum and dad."

"I'm sure you do," Janie said comfortingly.

"Once Christmas dinner is over the family tend to look after themselves and we're free to do what we want," June continued chattily as she fluffed up the pillows behind Janie's back and handed her the cup of tea. "My boyfriend lives just down the road a way in the next town. I'm going there later."

"You obviously like it here," Janie said quietly.

"Oh, I love it, miss," June said warmly. "Mr Steel's smashing to work for and it's a real happy house. Not like some my mates are in—the things I could tell you..." She raised expressive eyes to the ceiling.

Janie was disconcerted to find that she was faintly annoyed at the effusive praise. She had never put herself down as small-minded and it was galling to recognise that she would have been happier to find that Kane was something of an ogre at home. What on earth is the matter with me? she thought irritably as June breezed out of the room to fetch her breakfast tray. It wasn't like her to be churlish or querulous. Of course the man would have a few good points; even the worst villains throughout history had had something good in their make-up.

It was as though it frightened her to accept he had

a softer side, her mind churned on as she sipped the hot, sweet tea, because that might open other doors she would prefer to keep closed. Of course that wasn't it! She repudiated the idea fiercely even as it took form, and if she didn't stop this mental cross-examination she always seemed to indulge in whenever her mind veered in his direction she would send herself crazy! It would seem she was here for today at least, and owing to circumstances which had been *completely* out of her control, she told herself quickly, and the logical thing to do was to take each minute, each hour as it came and to try to emerge unscathed from the lion's den.

"Good morning." It was the King of the Beasts himself and the colour flared savagely into her face as he stood lazily in the doorway, his dark face clean-shaven and undeniably attractive. "I looked in earlier but you were still asleep," he continued casually as he sauntered slowly into the room, his eyes faintly narrowed against the bright winter sunshine streaming into the room and his big body relaxed and at ease. "It's a beautiful day outside—the storms are all over."

"Are they?" Not this roaring tempest inside of me, she thought breathlessly as he stopped at the end of the bed, his dark face inscrutable. He was devastatingly casual in jeans and a white polo-neck sweater, and the way the clothes sat on his tall, lean figure would have boosted the sales sky-high in any advertisement. "How long have I been asleep?"

"Well, it's ten o'clock now, so I make that about

thirteen hours," he said lightly. "You look much better. How do you feel?"

"Fine." She smiled warily. "I still can't believe I'm here, actually."

"Neither can I." His voice was deep and cool and there wasn't a trace of amusement in the rugged face. "Do you regret it?"

She stared at him silently as she wondered how to reply. Yes, she regretted it, with every fibre of her being! She was in the middle of something that seemed to have galloped away out of her control and the knowledge was frightening. She was drawn to him physically in a way she had never experienced before and wouldn't have thought possible outside of storybooks, and every excited beat of her heart, every tremble in her stomach was a brutal betrayal of her father, the worst sort of treachery there could be.

"Kane—"

"No, don't say it." He held up a large hand as an expression of dry cynicism replaced the strange waiting look glittering in the blue eyes. "I don't want you to lie to me and the truth would be too crushing. Your face said it all anyway. I'm suitably chastened." She didn't quite understand the laconic, wry mockery and she stared at him wide-eyed as he seated himself in the chair he had occupied the night before. "And don't look so tragic, sweetheart; it makes a nice change to be the hunter rather than the hunted."

"What?" She had lost the thread somewhere, she thought, only half listening to the slow, drawling voice as she struggled to come to terms with what his nearness was doing to her body.

"Drink your tea." He nodded towards the half-full cup in her hands. "June is bringing you a light breakfast in a moment and lunch is at one. Do you think you'll be able to come downstairs to eat?"

"Of course I will." His immaculate appearance was making her feel even more dishevelled and she raised a hand to her tousled hair as she spoke. "I'll try and make myself more presentable," she added as she set the empty cup on the bedside cabinet.

"You look perfect just as you are." He leant forward suddenly and stroked the silky curve of her face with the tip of a finger. "My little prisoner." As he moved to lean over her she knew, with a burst of blazing disloyalty, that she had been hoping he would kiss her from the moment he had come into the room and, as his lips found hers, what had been meant as a gentle caress rapidly turned into something passionate and fierce. She heard him groan deep in his throat as his hands went round her to pull her more closely against him, and then he was sitting on the bed with her body moulded against his hardness and his mouth devouring hers. And the awful thing was that she didn't want him to stop, she thought with a surge of horror. She knew it was her response that was triggering this fire in him, but she couldn't hide what he was doing to her any more than she could stop breathing.

It was the sound of his name being called from downstairs that stopped the madness, the intrusion causing his body to stiffen for a second before he stood up abruptly and walked straight out of the room without a word. She stared after him blankly, her senses rushing and her body aflame with mortifying shame and humiliation. How could she? How *could* she have done that? she asked herself in stunned amazement. It wasn't even as if she was used to falling into a man's arms at a moment's notice, although he would never believe that now, she thought bleakly. Three years in the free and easy atmosphere of university had made her evaluate her personal moral code at an early age and, although some of her closest friends had been able to fall in and out of bed with every boyfriend on the first date, she had known that was not for her. She wouldn't have been able to give herself and then just walk away with a smile and no trace of regret—she wasn't made that way—and once she had come to terms with how she felt it had been easy to live her life accordingly. But then she had never met anyone like him, her mind jabbed at her sharply; she had never known that a man could possess such sensual power.

"Here we are, miss." As June breezed happily into the room, her pretty face aglow, Janie forced a quick smile to her face and took the tray containing toast, scrambled eggs and freshly squeezed orange juice from the maid with a quick nod of thanks.

"That looks lovely, thank you," she said quietly.

"Mrs Langton didn't want to spoil your appetite for dinner," June explained quickly, "so there isn't much. Would you like me to run you a bath while you eat or would you prefer a shower?"

"A bath, I think, please," Janie said gratefully. The thought of soaking away the effects of the last few days in a tub of warm, scented water was irresistible.

"Right you are." As the young girl bustled away into the adjoining bathroom Janie bit into a slice of warm toast and reflected that there was something to be said for gracious living, especially when one was recovering from flu. She would have to be on her guard, she thought wryly. This whole set-up was definitely a lure to an ordinary working girl like herself. And that *was* all she was. Whatever had prompted Kane Steel to call round the night before, whether it was a desire for revenge or maybe this strange physical attraction that was too real to be denied, there was no way any relationship between them could work. Even friendship was out. The past was still too painful and he wasn't the sort of man a girl like her got involved with, she knew that. A vivid picture of the ethereal blonde she had seen him with on that first night swam starkly into her mind. She had neither the looks, the wealth nor the poise to compete with beauties like that, and she didn't intend to anyway! He might be the most attractive man she had ever met in her life, but his darker side eclipsed the fatal charm entirely and *that* was what she had to concentrate on.

She had probably dented that powerful egoism that was an essential part of any male, she thought later as she lay soaking in the warm bath in a cloud of expensively perfumed bubbles. It *had* been all-out war from the first moment they had met and perhaps this interest he seemed to be displaying in her was an attempt to subject her to his will, to forge a link that he could use to subdue and tame her. Yes, that was it. She sat up suddenly in the silky water. Of *course* that was it.

"Well, it won't work, Mr Steel," she said loudly into the empty room. "I'm nobody's fool and I'm not taken in by this softly, softly approach for a second." She glanced at herself a few minutes later when she stepped out of the bath, critically running over her face and figure in the big-mirrored wall that ran the length of the bathroom. Not bad, she thought with analytical impartiality, but there's nothing to drive a man wild with passion, is there? Especially not a hard, ruthless multi-millionaire with an eye for the ladies and a lifestyle that could easily feature in the more glossy magazines.

She dressed slowly, finding she was shakier than she had thought, drying her hair carefully as she sat at the huge ornate dressing-table and letting it fall in soft, silky curls to her shoulders. The dress that Kane had packed for her was a light wool fabric in soft gold that she had only bought recently, and the chic cut made her look taller and slimmer than she really was. "You cost me an arm and a leg," she said soberly to the gold reflection in the mirror, "but you were worth every penny." She shut her eyes for a moment as her head swam and then cleared. When she got home tonight she would hibernate for a couple of days until she was completely back to normal. If she could just get through the next few hours without courting disaster...

"Janie..." It had seemed to take her an age to make

her way downstairs and she was fighting the temptation to be completely overawed with every ounce of will-power she possessed. This was just a house, he was just a man, his family were just flesh-and-blood people... Kane moved immediately to her side as she walked hesitantly into the vast drawing-room where she had been an unwilling guest that first night. "I'm glad you joined us, but you look very pale; come and sit by the fire and I'll introduce you to everyone."

At her first nervous glance the huge room had seemed to be full of people, but once she was sitting down with a glass of sherry in her hand, and Kane perched on the arm of the chair at her side, she realised that, besides Kane, there were only three other adults and two small children present.

"Mother and Father." Kane indicated the elderly good-looking couple seated side by side on a two-seater settee an arm stretch away. "And the two little angels in the corner are not so angelic once you get to know them." He grinned at the children who grinned back immediately. "Christopher and Charlotte and their mother, Tina, my brother's family." Tina nodded her head unsmilingly, her cool face holding just the right amount of reserve to remind Janie that she was a stranger in their midst.

Kane's parents were both gracious and friendly, absorbing her into the general conversation as though she had known them all for years as they chatted about this and that and played with the children, who were extremely well-behaved for such tiny tots.

"Have you known Kane long?" Tina asked suddenly in a lull in the conversation, looking directly at Janie for the first time, her carefully made-up blue eyes as sharp as honed steel. The question caught Janie by surprise and, as she stared back into the other woman's flawless, aristocratic face framed by its halo of sleek blonde hair cut expensively into an exquisitely shaped bob, she realised, quite abruptly, that Keith's wife had taken an instant dislike to her.

"No, not long," she replied quietly, holding the tight blue gaze without flinching until the other woman lowered her eyes to the long-stemmed wine glass in her pale, manicured hand.

"Where did you meet?" Tina raised her head again as she took a sip of wine and the diamond studs in her ears flashed brilliantly in the bright sunlight filtering into the warm room, the elegant, finely cut suit in raw silk that she wore so casually screaming an exclusive price label. "Kane gets about all over the place, don't you, darling?" The blue gaze didn't soften as it rested on her brother-in-law's dark face.

What was all this about? Janie thought curiously as she felt Kane stiffen beside her. As she opened her mouth to reply, Kane was there before her, his deep, rich voice bland and smooth with the merest hint of an edge to it as he looked directly at Tina's beautiful face. "We met at a conference," he said quietly, "about three weeks ago, wasn't it, darling?" As his eyes swung down to her she gazed up at him for a long moment in amazement. Darling? *Darling*! "And then when Janie was taken ill it seemed logical for her

to spend some time here.'' The hard hand on her arm
warned her to keep quiet.

''I should think so, too,'' his mother said comfortably. ''You live by yourself, don't you, Janie?''

''Yes.'' She smiled into the lined but still lovely
face in front of her, grateful for the diversion. She'd
have a word with Kane later about this ''darling' business and the impression he seemed to have given his
family regarding his relationship with her. How *dared*
he act as though she was his girlfriend?

As the talk swung back on to safer topics she was
aware of Tina's hard gaze burning into the side of her
head, and when she turned to meet the other woman's
eyes they were full of naked hostility as they moved
slowly and deliberately down her body, mentally cal-
culating the cost of her dress and hairstyle. As the
finely shaped mouth drew up slightly at one side in an
unmistakable little sneer Janie felt herself flush hotly
at the purposeful snub. What an unpleasant woman,
she thought angrily as she turned back to answer
something Kane's mother had asked. What a thoroughly unpleasant woman. The sooner she was out of
this place the better. She was unaware that a second
pair of ice-cold eyes had been watching the little
exchange, their blueness glacial.

''Shall we go through to the dining-room?'' Kane
asked smoothly after a few more minutes had elapsed,
and Janie noticed, as they all left the drawing-room,
that he bent down and murmured something quietly in
Tina's ear that sent the blonde's cool, remote face an
ugly shade of puce, before returning to Janie's side

and taking her arm as they followed the others from the room.

''What did you say to her?'' Janie asked directly as they stood for a second in the huge hall, the others having disappeared into the dining-room. ''It was something to do with me, wasn't it?''

''What sharp little eyes you have,'' he said unemotionally, indicating the dining-room with a wave of his hand. ''Come along.''

''What was it?'' she persisted obstinately, remaining stock-still as he made to start walking again. ''I want to know.''

He looked down at her, with a mixture of exasperation and amusement turning the blue eyes brilliant, and sighed with exaggerated patience as he shook his head slowly. ''What an obstinate little mule you are, sweetheart.'' His warm, lazy voice turned the words into a compliment rather than an insult. ''I can see I'm not going to get away with a thing where you're concerned.'' She didn't answer but remained staring up into his dark face until he bowed with mocking capitulation. ''Yes, it was about you,'' he said slowly. ''Satisfied?''

''No.'' She held his gaze defiantly. ''You haven't told me what yet.''

''I merely warned the lady to keep her acid tongue under control where you are concerned,'' he said mildly. ''I suggested it might put a damper on the festive season if I was forced to pack her off home, that's all.''

''That's all?'' She remembered Tina's cold, superior face and beautiful, cutting eyes and felt a moment's grudging respect for Kane's nerve. "That's quite a lot! She's rather daunting, isn't she?"

"Tina?" He was frankly amazed. "She's just a spoilt little daddy's girl who has yet to realise what life is all about despite being widowed with two children. The world is full of nasty little cats like her, Janie. Unfortunately my brother chose to fall in love with that particular one and therefore..." He shrugged eloquently. "But she toes the line with me or expects the consequences."

"I see." She didn't quite know what to say next.

"Matter closed?" he asked quietly and she nodded quickly. "Good. Come along, then; no doubt Mrs Langton is champing at the bit because we aren't ready and waiting. Now she *is* a daunting lady!"

As they entered the dining-room, the huge table a vision of Christmas extravagance beautifully decorated in festal colours of green, red and gold, Janie was reminding herself yet again just how astute and perceptive this man was. She doubted if any of the others had noticed Tina's antagonism, but he had, instantly, and had just as instantly dealt with it. How could she believe he hadn't had anything to do with her father's disastrous transaction or at least had some knowledge of the ruthless negotiations? The acquisition of their business had enabled the whole block to come under the ownership of Steel Enterprises, which had turned it into a very important deal, important enough to cost her father his life. And yet... Would he lie to her so cold-bloodedly? She glanced at him under her eyelashes as they took their places at the table. She didn't know; she just didn't know. She noticed, as Kane was sitting down, that he moved awkwardly and something akin to a flash of pain seared across the rugged features for a brief instant. His mother, seated on his right, put her hand on his arm in an unspoken question and he smiled at her as he settled himself in the seat, patting her hand as he shook his head slightly.

Another mystery? She felt a moment of irritation. Didn't anyone come right out and say what they wanted to in this house?

"Janie?" She suddenly realised that Kane's father had been speaking to her and she hadn't heard a word.

"I'm sorry?" She smiled apologetically.

"I asked how you are faring in handling this son of mine," he said comfortably. "You have to watch him, you know."

"Yes." Her firm voice carried more honesty than tact and he blinked slightly at her vehemence. "I do know."

"Good." He recovered quickly. "Good."

"You could say I've met my match at long last." Kane's deep voice joined the conversation with dry, sardonic amusement. "Isn't that right, sweetheart?"

As she met his eyes over the table she saw that although his face was smiling and outwardly amused, giving an impression of dry indulgence, the dark fire burning in the hard eyes was far from convivial. He had heard the exchange and hadn't liked it, she conjectured quickly. Good! Just so long as he got the message. She shrugged lightly without answering, turning to his father and asking how old the children were. They had been whisked upstairs some time ago by the capable June, Tina announcing to the room in general that it was "just *too* tiresome to have them eat with the adults and they needed a nap anyway".

The meal was quite delicious, starting with consommé *chasseur*, a light, clear soup consisting of cooked game and good port wine, garnished with tiny strips of cooked vegetables known as *julienne*, followed by the traditional turkey with all the trimmings and finishing with a huge plum pudding heavily doused with brandy and lashings of thick double cream. By the time she had finished, Janie felt as though she could hardly move. It was the first real meal she had eaten in days, and she suddenly felt so tired, it was an effort to put one leg in front of the other as they walked through to the drawing-room after coffee.

She was stifling her third yawn in as many minutes when Kane's mother leant across and touched her hand gently. "Why don't you go and have a nap, my dear?" she said softly. "You don't want to overdo it. Flu needs to be treated with respect."

"Would you mind?" Janie included the whole room in the sweep of her head. "I do feel ridiculously tired."

"Not at all." Kane answered for all of them, his voice bland. "I'll come and tuck you in in a minute." She eyed him tightly without answering; that little gibe had been retribution for her conversation with his father earlier. His parents laughed easily at what they considered Kane's little joke, but not so Tina—she sent a glance of pure venom Janie's way, and as Janie rose she was conscious that the other woman was watching her every move, her gaze only breaking away when the children bounded into the room, their small round faces still flushed with sleep and as bright as buttons.

"Can you find the way to your room?" Kane had followed her to the foot of the stairs and as she turned to reply she saw that he was holding a thin rectangular parcel in his hand, beautifully wrapped in festive gold paper. "For you." He had placed it in her hand before she could gather her wits. "We exchanged presents very early this morning—Christopher and Charlotte saw to that." He smiled ruefully. "Five o'clock, if you want the gory details."

"But…" She stared at him helplessly. "How could you have…? You didn't know I was coming. I haven't got anything for anyone."

"Of course you haven't," he said comfortably. "As it happens, this belonged to my grandmother and I would like you to have it."

"Your grandmother?" She stared down at the slender package for a moment as though it were alive. "I can't possibly accept anything that belonged to your grandmother, Kane; you know I can't. I hardly know you…"

"Does that matter?" he asked lazily, the intentness of his gaze belying the drawling voice.

"Of course it matters." She shook her head slightly

at the absurdness of the situation. "Your parents wouldn't like—"

"My parents have nothing to do with this," he said quietly but with a thread of steel in the softness. "And you don't even know what it is yet."

As she carefully tore the paper and opened the long box his eyes were tight on her, and as she lifted the cobweb-thin gold chain holding a tiny gold star in which nestled a small blood-red ruby he spoke again, his voice soft and deep.

"It isn't very valuable. My maternal grandfather was a poor farm lad when he met my grandmother, whose parents owned half of Ireland. They courted in secret for a year and he saved most of his wage each week for months to buy her the pendant on her eighteenth birthday. It proved to be the catalyst which revealed their relationship to her parents and ultimately led to their marriage—after many months of heartache and pain, I might add. Her parents had apparently got some lord or earl lined up for her. My grandfather was a poor substitute in their eyes."

"And in your grandmother's eyes?" she asked softly, fascinated by the story.

"They loved each other till the day they died," he said just as softly. "She had diamonds and furs and jewellery that had been in the family for generations, but I never saw her with anything but a plain gold band on the third finger of her left hand and the pendant round her neck."

She stared at him aghast now, her eyes wide and troubled. "But you can't possibly give it to me with a history like that; it's far too precious," she said urgently. "Your mother—"

"Will understand perfectly when I explain to her that I wanted to give you a Christmas gift," he interrupted smoothly, his face closing and his eyes suddenly veiled as he turned and walked back across the hall towards the drawing-room.

"But Kane—" Her voice was lost as he closed the door firmly after him, but she knew he had heard her, and as she stared down at the delicate little star her stomach turned over in panic. She didn't understand this, she didn't understand any of it, but female intuition told her she was in way over her head.

What did it all mean? As she climbed the stairs to her room her thoughts were spinning. Did the history of the pendant mean anything to him? It must do, surely; the way in which he had related it was so…personal, so intimate. But if it did, why had he given it to her of all people? She paused at the door to her rooms and shook her head slightly. Or maybe he regarded it as merely an item of jewellery, of little intrinsic value and therefore suitable as a gift to someone he barely knew? But that wasn't it. She *knew* that wasn't it.

Once in the bedroom she virtually collapsed on the bed, her tired mind heavy and dull. This was all a dream, a strange, crazy dream where people did and said unfathomable things that would melt away in the light of day. She looked again at the inoffensive pendant and then started violently as a large shape suddenly jumped up on to the bed beside her. "Juniper…

You scared me half to death.'' The big tabby cat blinked lazily as he curled up beside her and she smiled ruefully as Cosmos, a slightly smaller version of the striped feline, joined his father on the bed, purring loudly.

Mrs Langton's strict rule was no animals upstairs. She'd really have to shoo them out in a minute, she thought heavily as the warm bodies snuggled into her side, soft and furry like live teddy bears. She was asleep the next second, one arm unconsciously cuddling Juniper into her and the other flung over her head, still holding the pendant tightly in her hand.

She was unaware of a tall, dark figure coming into the room a few minutes later to stand watching her silently for long, taut moments. Juniper and Cosmos raised gleaming eyes for a moment, relaxing again when they saw that their master was more interested in their companion than in them, their soft purring indicating that they found the situation very satisfactory.

Before he left, Kane threw the coverlet off the other bed over Janie's sleeping form, half burying the cats in the process, who remained stock-still, determined to leave only under protest, and as he bent down and brushed her lips lightly with his own he sighed, the sound deep and hard and seeming to come from the very depths of him as he glanced again at the pendant, delicate and bright and shining in her relaxed fingers.

# CHAPTER SIX

THE room was filled with shadows when Janie opened her eyes, the cats long since gone. She lay for a moment in the warm darkness, wondering what had woken her, until the knock on the door was repeated.

"Yes? Come in." As she swung her feet over the side of the bed Baines's head popped round the half-open door.

"Excuse me, miss, sorry to wake you, but I wondered if you'd like these in here?" He came fully into the room and she saw he was carrying her other suitcase and the large flight bag she used for overnight visits.

"I'm sorry?" She stared at him vacantly.

"Your things, miss. I thought I'd leave them in here. Bit heavy for you to carry through," the chauffeur said cheerfully.

"My things?" A flood of anger swept through her as realisation dawned. "What are they doing here? Who told you—?"

"I did." The cold, deep voice brought both sets of eyes snapping round to the relaxed figure in the doorway and Baines put the bags on the floor before leaving quietly and quickly, his face carefully blank.

"You told him to go and get my clothes from the flat?" She glared into Kane's expressionless face, her eyes fiery. "You know I'm leaving tonight!"

"You aren't well enough." He moved into the room, his steps indolent and unhurried, seemingly unaffected by her rage.

"I'll be the judge of that," she said furiously. "If I wanted a strange man poking about among my belongings—"

"Mrs Langton packed the clothes and only from the wardrobe you mentioned to me on Christmas Eve," he said shortly. "My employees are not in the habit of having light fingers, if that's what's worrying you."

"Of course it's not that!" She had never known anyone who could make her so mad so quickly, she reflected angrily as she stared into the cool blue eyes. "I'm sure they are all completely trustworthy and I haven't got anything worth taking anyway."

"Good. End of problem." He smiled sardonically, his mouth hard.

"I could hit you." She glared at him furiously.

"Again?" He touched his cheek with his hand, his mouth still smiling, but his eyes as cold as ice. "I wouldn't recommend it, Janie. Once was a mistake, twice would be…most unfortunate."

"You had no right to bring my things here." She almost stamped her foot like an angry child, but stopped herself just in time. He was so damnably smug! "You agreed I'd leave tonight—"

"I did no such thing." He leant back against the wall, folding his arms and narrowing his eyes as he watched her mounting rage with what looked like cool interest. ''I might have mentioned you could leave when you were well enough, which you aren't. In case you've forgotten, it was only this time yesterday that you passed out on me most thoroughly and you told me yourself you haven't been eating properly in the last few days. You are physically exhausted and all but burnt out and there is no way I'm allowing you to go home to an empty building until you are well and truly over this thing—so you may as well resign yourself to the fact.''

''Your conscience would bother you?'' she asked tightly with heavy sarcasm.

''Something like that.'' He eyed her expressionlessly.

''I don't believe you've got one!'' She had never felt so utterly helpless in all her life and the urge to lash out was paramount. ''Or if you have it's a very convenient little piece of equipment, isn't it, switched on and off just when it suits you?''

''Don't be tiresome.'' As he covered the few feet to her side and pulled her to her feet she stiffened instinctively. ''I don't intend to stand here and engage in such a futile conversation when I can think of a far more interesting pastime.''

''I warned you before—''

''So you did.'' He cut off her words by the simple expedient of placing his lips on hers as he imprisoned her in his arms, his height and breadth dwarfing her small frame and the sheer maleness of his hard body deliciously tantalising.

She *had* to fight him this time. The message burnt into her nervous system and as her limbs obeyed the call to arms she began to struggle and twist, turning her head from side to side in an effort to avoid his searching mouth.

"Be still." The muttered words against her face held an inexcusable note of amusement. How dared he find this humorous, how *dared* he? she thought hotly as she freed her hands from her side and began to beat against the rock-hard chest with all her might.

"I hate you. You know that, don't you?" she spat angrily as he effortlessly enclosed her wrists in one great fist, holding them securely behind her back.

"Maybe." There was no trace of laughter in the deep voice now, just a thick husky hunger that joined with something deep inside her to produce an actual shudder that ran through her body like fire.

"I do," she said raggedly, looking at his mouth as it descended on hers with a sense of doomed helplessness. How could she fight him and herself? she thought desperately as his tongue pillaged the secret places of her inner mouth with arrogant force, causing a trembling in her body that was impossible to hide. But she had to, she *had* to; she just couldn't think why when he was so close. The heavily muscled arms and shoulders, the big, broad chest that spoke of lean, hard power, the mesmerising maleness that oozed out of every pore and tissue—it was too potent, too compelling...

She was crushed against him now, his lips devouring her mouth, her throat, his hands running over her body with a knowledge that brought fire into her limbs and a trembling deep in her stomach that spread hot warmth through every vein. As he gently lowered her on to the bed she couldn't resist; every part of her had melted into him, and he was the only real thing in this spinning kaleidoscope of touch and taste and smell.

She made a small sound of protest as he unzipped her dress, folding the soft material off her limbs in one swift movement that spoke of an expertise that only fully dawned on her much later, but now his hands were stroking along the silky flesh only partly covered by the thin ivory silk slip she was wearing, and, again, nothing else mattered but the feel of his body against hers.

"You're delicious, absolutely delicious, do you know that...?" As he pulled her close against him, moulding her softness into the powerful contours of his body, she felt the hard ridge that swelled tightly against his clothing and spoke of his arousal more loudly than any words. She stiffened, suddenly panic-stricken as harsh reality flooded in like an icy cold deluge. What was she doing? What on *earth* was she doing? She'd taken leave of her senses. To invite this, and with him?

He sensed her withdrawal immediately and made no effort to cajole her as she feared, turning over instead to swing his feet over the side of the bed and run his fingers through his springy black hair before rising slowly.

"You'll stay for a day or two?" he asked huskily as he turned to face her, and for a moment the look on his face made her dumb. She had expected triumph, satisfaction, perhaps even annoyance or irritation at the sudden termination of their lovemaking, but this expression that was twisting the rugged features was none of those things. Just what it was she couldn't fathom, but it was devastatingly seductive. "I promise you this won't happen again. It wasn't planned, Janie, do you believe that?"

"I don't know." She shook her head slightly as her cheeks burnt red. The only thing she was sure about at the moment was that she wasn't sure about anything! This thing that seemed to leap into life between them as soon as their bodies touched was fierce and potent, but how was she to know if it affected him the way it did her, whether it was under his control and being used for his own purposes? He was capable of great ruthlessness and an objectivity with regard to other human beings which was quite alien to her. This could all be a game to him. He was rich enough, and probably spoilt enough, to fancy a little diversion with someone as unworldly as herself, a change from his usual diet of graceful cool blondes and exquisitely dressed model-types.

"You'll stay till Sunday." Suddenly the tone was different and her hackles rose immediately at the authoritative note. "My family will think it strange if you suddenly dash off now, besides which my mother is looking forward to having you around a little longer. She doesn't get on too well with Tina." His eyes were hooded and hidden from her, his mouth hard.

"I can't imagine why," Janie said sarcastically as

she pulled the duvet around her with as much non-chalance as she could muster considering she was half naked and he was as cool as a cucumber. "And for the record I'm not here to do you any favours regarding your mother or anything else. When I think of how you treated my father—"

"Look on it as pouring burning coals on my head, then, if that makes you feel better," he said coldly, his eyes ice-blue and totally without warmth.

"Wouldn't it be simpler all round if I just left?" Janie asked with a trace of bewilderment in her voice. "I don't understand why you want me to stay. It was kind of you to act the Good Samaritan, but there's no need—"

"Maybe you were right in the first place—a guilty conscience or something similar." He moved towards the door, his face closed and dark, and for a moment she could see why he was so successful in such a cut-throat world. He was frightening. Was this really the same man who had held her close just a few minutes before, murmuring words of passion and doing things to her that she had never imagined were possible? "Dinner is at eight."

The door had closed behind him before she could react and she stared into the empty room stupidly, her emotions a churning mass of anger, irritation, helpless frustration at her own vulnerability and something else…something she didn't dare dwell on for even a moment because somehow, in spite of all that had happened, all she knew about him, in the deep recesses of her heart she wanted to stay, and that was what was terrifying her beyond coherent thought.

"Janie...are you rested?" Kane's mother was immediately at her side as she entered the drawing-room later that evening where the others were enjoying pre-dinner drinks. The atmosphere was relaxed and graceful, the surroundings luxurious and beautiful and the people elegant, and Janie had never wanted to be somewhere else so desperately.

She had dressed carefully, blessing the fact that the advertising world in which she lived had necessitated several good and expensive outfits for evening functions, and now, as she glanced at the other two women, she knew her choice of evening wear had been appropriate. The simple classical lines of the expertly cut "original" little black dress complemented her curves and deepened the rich brown of her eyes and, combined with the upswept hairstyle softened by the odd tendril of hair curling alluringly against her white skin, the whole effect was one of subtle sophistication.

She smiled at Kane's mother as she nodded quietly. "Yes, thank you. I'm sorry I seem to be so feeble at the moment. I'm never ill normally."

"Flu is no respecter of the norm." Mr Steel smiled easily as he joined his wife at Janie's side. "Now, what would you like to drink? I'm doing the honours at the moment."

"Kane's not here?" She glanced round the room quickly.

"Phone call from the States that couldn't be ignored,'' his mother said with a touch of asperity. "Or so he said.'' The soft blue eyes looked straight into Janie's brown ones. "He needs taking in hand, my dear, taught to let go a bit. He has never been very good at delegating and he works far too hard. Especially—'' She stopped abruptly as Kane's father coughed warningly. "Well, you know what I mean,'' she finished lamely.

Yes, I think I probably do, Janie thought tightly as she forced a non-committal smile past the sudden flood of bitterness darkening her eyes. "Never very good at delegating'', and from the horse's mouth—or the horse's mother's mouth, she corrected silently. She'd just bet he wasn't, she had known that from the start, and he honestly expected her to believe he hadn't been involved with her father's take-over?

"On Christmas Day, too,'' his mother nattered on, blithely unaware of Janie's barely concealed anger. "It really isn't good enough. You should have a word with the boy, George.''

"I think Kane cut loose from the apron strings a good few years ago,'' his father returned drily as his eyes glinted with exasperation, "and I really don't think Janie wants to listen to you grumbling, my dear. Now, that drink?'' He turned to Janie with a warm smile.

"White wine if you have it, Mr Steel,'' Janie said politely and received a squeak of protest from his wife.

"Call us Aileen and George, dear,'' she said quickly. "Don't stand on ceremony.''

Janie had just taken a sip of wine, concentrating

with iron determination on ignoring the narrowed, cat-like stare from Tina, as Kane entered the room, and the jolt that went through her system totally unnerved her. The cool, remote blue eyes immediately sought her presence, resting on her face for a long moment before moving to the others in the room. "I hope you're all hungry. Mrs Langton seems to have excelled herself," he said easily as he walked lazily to Janie's side, and for a moment a picture of their bodies entwined on her bed flashed so vividly into her mind that the breath caught in her throat. This cold, austere man, fabulously wealthy and frighteningly powerful, had almost— She shut her eyes for an infinitesimal second. She wouldn't think of it. It had been a mistake that would not be repeated.

"You look quite beautiful." The soft, deep voice in her ear sent goose-pimples all over her body.

"Thank you." She didn't meet his eyes, trying for seasoned sophistication as she glanced somewhere in the region of his left ear.

"I could eat you alive." The whisper was for her ears alone and as her shocked brown eyes shot to meet his she saw that the dark face was wickedly bland, the import of his words only showing in the glittering heat burning in the depths of the narrowed eyes.

She pulled herself together with visible effort and smiled as coolly as she could, her voice dry. "You could *try*," she said with meaningful sarcasm, "but I can assure you you wouldn't get very far." He was going to show his true colours now, was he? she thought tightly as her mind raced crazily. The squire of the manor asserting his rights to acquire any maiden he so desired? Something along those lines? Well, this particular squire was in for a shock! She hadn't forgotten all his threats and she didn't trust him an inch.

"Spoilsport." He leaned forward to say more, but Tina's voice interrupted him from across the room where she had been sitting as straight as a ramrod, her face and body stiff and the beautiful eyes staring at Janie with terrifying intent.

"This nasty flu bug must have spoilt all your plans for Christmas," she said coldly with a little twist to her mouth that Janie didn't understand. "It was lucky you could drop everything when Kane arrived on your doorstep."

"Yes, I suppose so," Janie agreed with a touch of bewilderment in her voice. It was clear the beautiful blonde was trying to make a point of some kind, but just what it was eluded Janie for the moment.

"He called by chance?" Tina continued smoothly. "You didn't know he was coming?"

"No." Janie met the other woman's eyes firmly, but with the feeling that she was preparing to face an adversary blindfolded.

"I see." Tina opened her mouth to say more when Kane's father cut into the conversation, speaking directly to Kane.

"How did the call go?" he asked quietly. "Situation any better?"

"Not really," Kane answered shortly.

"Well, old Collins has got to face facts sooner or later," his father continued, seemingly unaware of

Kane's closed face. "His firm's finished; everyone knows it."

"Perhaps." Kane's voice was grim.

"His son might be a friend of yours, Kane, but Collins' empire is going to fold within weeks rather than months. Better you than one of the moguls who won't play fair. At least—"

"I don't think the women are interested in business, Dad," Kane said firmly as his father would have continued. "Let's change the subject."

"Oh, please..." Tina gave a hugely exaggerated sigh of distaste. "It's just too boring. If this silly little man has been stupid enough to lose his business it's his own fault and Kane has every right to move in, haven't you, darling...?" Her blue eyes were diamond-hard and as bright as crystal. "I just can't *bear* people who don't know when to give up; so embarrassing..."

"Tina—"

Kane's mother cut off his voice by rising swiftly and speaking loudly as she caught hold of his arm firmly. "It's eight o'clock, darling; Mrs Langton will be after us if we aren't in the dining-room in the next ten seconds. Come along, do." Kane looked down at his mother's softly imploring face for a long moment, the two of them communicating silently as she kept a tight grip on his arm, and then he sighed deeply as he gestured for the others to rise.

"Go through, everyone."

Janie stared at him as she remained sitting in her chair, the triteness of Tina's cruelty hitting a nerve that was still raw and bleeding. Was this how her father's business had been discussed, casually, coldly, as a little prelude to dinner? How could he let that woman be so callous, so heartless, without saying something? What was the matter with this family anyway? Didn't they realise that they were discussing the day-to-day lives of hundreds of ordinary folk who worked because they *had* to, because they needed to keep a roof over their heads? But they could treat the heartbreak involved quite abstractedly, after all, because they were safe and secure in this gold-lined palace. Well, enough was enough!

"I don't think I'm hungry." Janie's voice was clear and firm as she spoke straight into Kane's face before turning and glaring at Tina, who rose indolently to her feet. "Something seems to have ruined my appetite."

"We'll join you in a minute." Kane had ushered the others out of the room and shut the door almost before anyone could draw breath, and as he turned to face Janie again she saw that his eyes were veiled and cold, all emotion masked.

"I want to leave now, Kane." She faced him squarely, her eyes blazing. "You're all like aliens from another planet and I've had enough. How you can let Tina behave like that I'll never know. Whoever this Collins is, he's obviously desperate if he has to ring you on Christmas Day. What was he asking for, mercy?"

"Something like that," he said expressionlessly.

"But big business doesn't know the meaning of that word, does it?" she stated bitterly. "Well, I can't be a party to any more conversations like the one I just heard. It makes me feel…dirty, sick.''

''Not another word!'' The explosion, when it came, took her completely by surprise. One minute he had been standing watching her, his dark face still and unreadable, the next he had reached across with deadly intent to shake her roughly, his eyes murderous. She should have known, she thought fleetingly in the one timeless second before the onslaught came. The poker face was an invaluable business weapon which he had perfected to full advantage, but she had seen a glimpse of this other side of him that first night after the Press conference when the real Kane Steel had erupted in terrifying fury.

''You are going to shut up and sit still and listen to every word I say.'' He almost flung her into the chair she had just vacated, leaning over her menacingly, his hands resting on the arms of the chair and his face inches from hers. ''You talk about being sick? Well, I'm sick—sick of being cast in the role of big bad villain Kane, sick of seeing that look in your eyes every time something reminds you of your father, sick of you damn well not *listening* to me!''

She was listening now, she thought with chilling terror; she dared not do anything else. The black rage twisting the harsh features was raw and biting, its ferocity deadly.

''You talk about a conversation you've just heard. Are you totally stupid?'' he bit out angrily, his voice shaking. ''You listened to that black widow spider my brother married putting more venom into this room, that's what you *listened* to. Tina is the sort of woman who would have been burnt at the stake years ago. She's evil, believe me. From the moment she married my brother she humiliated him in the worst possible way, demeaning his manhood day in, day out. He was rich, but not rich enough. He was powerful, but not powerful enough. She wanted a hard, ruthless type who would whip her to within an inch of her life if she stepped out of line, and she got Keith instead. All he did, all he aimed for, was to be the sort of man she wanted him to be.''

"Kane—''

The brilliant eyes narrowed. ''I said shut up.'' She shut up. ''She despised him and he knew it, but he couldn't let go; he loved her.'' There was a bleakness in the harsh voice that spoke of unbearable pain.

''From a child he was gentle and tender and kind; you only had to see him with his children to understand that; they absolutely adored him. But those qualities spelt weakness to Tina and so he forced an image, cultivated a concept that destroyed him mentally and physically.''

''You hate her, don't you?'' Janie stared at him, her voice little more than a whisper.

''As I said, Keith loved her.'' He shrugged wearily, the anger dying as he looked into the past. ''And now he's gone there are the children. My mother lives for them. She couldn't believe it when her child died; it tore her apart, but caring for his children heals a little of the hurt day by day. And she has them often.'' His voice was bitter. ''Tina likes the high life and, besides being a rich widow, her own father is very wealthy and very powerful. If she took it into her head to move elsewhere, deny my parents visiting rights, it would be a long, hard, bitter fight through the courts to make it otherwise.''

"And she'd do that." Janie spoke almost to herself.

"Yes, she'd do that all right." He suddenly looked very tired as he sat down in the chair opposite. "The final bitter irony is that I was responsible for introducing them." As she looked deep into his face the urge to reach out and comfort him was so strong that she could taste it, an ache in her throat as she saw the undisguised pain on his face that almost stopped her breath. At the same time some instinct of self-preservation kept her motionless and silent, her hands clenched.

"Anyway, I thought you should be put in the picture before you judge my parents in the same way as Tina." He turned to her, his eyes hooded and bleak, unaware of her ambivalence. "My parents are good people; take it from me."

"You introduced them?" She forced herself to speak, to move, in an effort to stop the urge to take him in her arms that was growing second by second. She mustn't forget all the months of heartache, the damage this man and his organisation had wrought in her family; it would be sheer suicide, but...somehow she found all the reasoning melting away in the face of his naked agony. She had never thought to see him so open, so vulnerable and it pierced something deep inside that actually caused a physical ache in her chest.

He nodded slowly, leaning back in the chair wearily and shutting his eyes. "I'd met her a few months before at a rather grand luncheon her father had taken her to. Business and pleasure, you know." Janie didn't, but made the appropriate response. "We had a drink together once or twice after that, a theatre date, and then *finito*."

"I see." The sick feeling in the pit of her stomach was as unwelcome as it was surprising.

"Keith and I were dining out one night after a long, involved business deal—I was trying to amalgamate him into the company as his own career had just taken a nosedive—and Tina came across to our table. They seemed to hit it off immediately. She was charm itself." His mouth curled scathingly.

"And you didn't mind?" she asked carefully as her heart pounded painfully.

"What?" He opened his eyes now, straightening in the chair slowly. "Mind? Why the hell should I mind? She was just a casual acquaintance as far as I was concerned, one of those ships that pass in the night. I was surprised she was my brother's type once he'd got to know her, though—until Tina our taste in women had been quite compatible. I thought he'd see—"

"See?" she prompted him as he stopped abruptly.

"See her for what she is," he finished quietly, with a tight shrug of his broad shoulders.

"The way you did." Suddenly it all fell into place and as she stared across at the attractive, rugged face opposite her Janie felt a moment's piercing amazement that this astute, clever man couldn't see what was under his very nose. Tina had fallen for Kane Steel, desperately. The barely concealed hostility at another young woman being brought into his house at Christmas when she had expected a cosy family tête-à-tête, the obvious dissatisfaction with life in general and her treatment of his brother when he had been alive, it all boiled down to the fact that she had married the wrong man and she knew it. What had prompted her to marry Keith when she had wanted his brother? Janie felt a flash of very real bewilderment at the duplicity of human beings. Had it been to enable her to stay near Kane? To live on the perimeter of his life if she couldn't be the central point? And Keith. Had he had any idea that the mould Tina had been trying to force him into was a caricature of his older brother—dominating, powerful, ruthless and, to Tina, fascinating? And Kane had said *she* was tangled in a dark web! she thought ironically.

"Well, now you know." For a moment she thought he had read her mind and then she realised he was referring to his revelation about the state of his brother's marriage and why the family tolerated Tina now. Maybe Kane had known how Tina felt? She looked at his dark face closely. It was impossible to tell; he was as imperturbable as always.

"No one will convince me that she didn't break him eventually, but there's not a damn thing I can do about it. I don't know how much Keith told my mother when he was alive, but I doubt it was much, if anything. He only confided in me towards the end when he was desperate."

"But at least you were around to listen," she said quickly.

"Only because—" He stopped abruptly. "Yes, I guess so." She looked at him searchingly. He had been about to say something else, she was sure of it. "The hell of it is, he never stopped loving her," Kane said bleakly. He shook his head slowly as he held her troubled brown eyes with his own blue ones. "Can you understand a love like that?"

"Can you?" She knew it was the coward's way out, but for some reason she couldn't answer his question. It had caused such a flood of panic to race through her system that she felt almost faint.

"Yes." There was a tenseness about him that was reflected in his voice. "Heaven help me, I can."

They sat unmoving for long moments, their eyes locked, before he moved to kneel on the carpet in front of her, taking her in his arms with a desperation that shocked her.

His mouth was urgent and hungry on hers, his breathing ragged, and for a moment Janie felt as though she was being torn to pieces with the conflicting emotions that shot through her. She wanted to think of him as completely cruel and ruthless, *needed* to—it was the only defence she had—but he kept getting in the way. The thought of any relationship with him, any at all, was a leap into the unknown of such magnitude that she couldn't face it and yet... What if she was wrong? Just *supposing* she was wrong? And then, as suddenly as he had kissed her, she was free.

"You'll have dinner?" He had risen to stand, looking down at her, that mask that he wore so often slipping into place even as she glanced up at him. She took the hand he offered, her head whirling as they walked through to join the others at the magnificent table, and just for a moment, as they sat down, she caught Tina's gaze. Her eyes were full of such malevolence, such naked jealousy, that it was confirmation of all Janie's suspicions, but then the carefully darkened eyelids blanketed the venom as the other woman looked down at her wine glass, her blonde hair swinging like a curtain over her pale cheeks.

The food was cooked to perfection, but Janie didn't taste a thing, eating, talking and smiling mechanically, her thoughts centred on the big dark man seated at the head of the table. This thing that she had recognised tonight was like a time bomb, an unstable, volatile volcano just waiting to go off and destroy this whole family. It was clear that Kane had loved his brother very much. She glanced at his face as he smiled dutifully at one of his father's long jokes. What would happen if Tina ever admitted to the twisted motives behind her treatment of her husband? How would he cope with that?

Stop it, Janie, she thought angrily after Kane's mother had had to repeat something twice to get her attention. This is nothing to do with you—*he* is nothing to do with you. Stop thinking about him; none of this matters. But it did. She didn't want him hurt. The knowledge brought her brown eyes wide open for a split-second as she shook herself mentally. Oh, she'd have to leave this place soon, very soon.

"Fancy a breath of fresh air?" Kane's voice was casual as they walked back into the drawing-room behind the others. "It might put the roses back in your cheeks."

"Now?" She stared at him in astonishment. "It's dark."

"So it is." He smiled mockingly. "But you can wrap up warm and the gardens are floodlit."

"OK," she agreed doubtfully. She didn't want to walk alone with him in the shadowed darkness, but neither could she face an hour or two of polite conversation with Tina's resentment colouring the very air she breathed. "But—" She stopped abruptly. There was no way she could put this without appearing either very gauche or provokingly hostile.

"But?" The ice-blue eyes held a satirical light. "I'm to be on my best behaviour, right?"

"Something like that." She raised her eyes to his defiantly. "That's not too much to ask, is it?"

"You'll never know." The tone was rueful with a deepness in the rich voice that made her tremble. "But—" He paused mockingly. "I'm sure this is good for my soul. Go and get your coat."

When she joined him in the hall a few minutes later he was standing waiting for her, his big body dark and dominating in the black overcoat he was wearing and his thick, springy hair shining in the light overhead. "Put this on." He handed her a grey cashmere scarf. "There's a heavy frost." As she wound the scarf round her neck the subtle scent of his aftershave reached out to jerk her senses into overdrive.

"Is this yours?" she asked abruptly.

"Yes." He looked at her in surprise. "Does that matter?"

"No." She lowered her eyes in confusion. This was driving her mad. *He* was driving her mad.

As they stepped out of the front door the sudden shock of the breathtakingly frosty air made her gasp slightly. They stood for a moment at the top of the steps, breathing in the cold, crisp sharpness after the cloying warmth of the house, and she saw that the trees and bushes were already clothed in wisps of white, magical under the dim lights that lit the garden. The night was beautifully clear, the sky a blanket of black velvet pierced with twinkling stars and flooded with a whispering stillness that held nature in a mystic, ethereal paleness.

"Isn't this better than the house?" Kane asked softly as he took her arm, threading it through his, and they began to walk.

"Yes." Her breath was a cloud of white in the icy air and she was very conscious of the height and breadth of him as they walked, his hard, dominant maleness somehow magnified in the pale, still world in which they strolled.

The grounds were beautifully laid out, the small narrow path winding through the rolling lawns dotted with trees surrounding the house leading, after a few minutes, to a large walled garden that was intricately designed with tiny shrubs, small trees and moss-covered terraced walls. "This is a wonderful place to sit in the summer," Kane said quietly as he indicated a tiny summer-house at the far end, partly hidden by an overhanging lilac tree. "Most of the shrubs are heavily perfumed and the bees and butterflies come from miles around to join our regular bird community."

"Do you come out here?" she asked in surprise. She hadn't thought of him as a connoisseur of nature in even the smallest way.

"You are determined not to accept that there could be anything good about me, aren't you?" The flat, expressionless way in which he spoke caused her to wonder for a brief moment if she had misheard the deep voice.

"Kane—"

"When are you going to let that shield down, just a fraction?" he asked softly as he turned her to face him, the moon a thin curve of light overhead. "You'll have to sooner or later, you know."

"Why?" She stared up at him, her eyes enormous in the shadowed garden.

"Because I never give up," he said simply. "I want you, Janie, you must know that, and I always get what I want."

"Always?" She couldn't read anything in the narrowed eyes looking down at her. "Surely not."

"Always." There wasn't a trace of humour in his face.

"No wonder you're so arrogant." She forced a note of hostility into her voice even as the sudden longing to rest her face against the broad chest reared its head.

"It's about time you realised that you're not omnipotent, Kane Steel."

"Is that why you aren't wearing it?" he asked quietly. "Another token of defiance?"

"What?" She stared at him for a second before realisation dawned. "Oh, you mean the pendant?"

He nodded, his lips curling with self-derisory amusement that didn't reach his cold eyes. "I mean the pendant," he affirmed softly.

"You must see I can't accept it," she said quickly as she tried to fathom what was going on behind that cool exterior. "Considering the history behind it, your grandmother and everything, you should never have given it to me."

"I'm getting a little tired of listening to what I should and shouldn't do," he said softly. "You really are a bossy little female, aren't you?" The last words were spoken more as a caress than a rebuke and in spite of herself a shiver of excitement trembled down her spine. It made her despise herself still more for that pervading weakness which took over the minute she was in his presence. Did all women react like this to him? She wouldn't be surprised; she wouldn't be surprised at all. No wonder his ego was colossal.

"Come here." His voice was thick and deep. "There's only one way I know to keep you quiet."

"No, Kane!" As he reached out to take her in his arms she sprang back so violently she almost fell. "I don't want you to touch me; I mean it."

"That's not the truth." He eyed her broodingly, his dark face a mass of craggy shadows in which the blue of his eyes glittered strangely. "It might be what your mouth is saying but your body tells me something quite different. You want me, Janie. Do us both a favour and admit it."

"You're so sure of yourself, aren't you?" The sheer arrogance of the man was breathtaking. "I suppose all your women collapse in your arms at the blink of an eye? Well, not this one. You do nothing for me except disgust me. I hate your lifestyle, your morals, everything about you, do you hear me?" She was conscious that she was forcing the defiance, the cruel words, past a growing weakness that was prompting her to give in to his demands. They were a talisman, a protection...

"Loud and clear." He leaned back against the gnarled trunk of an old bent apple tree as he watched her through hard, narrowed eyes. "And you mean to say that if I took you in my arms I couldn't have you willing within five minutes?"

"You're talking about sex," she said flatly, "and I don't doubt for a minute that you're an expert in that department." Not for a minute, she thought painfully.

He bent over in a small mocking bow. "A compliment?"

"It wasn't meant like that," she said weakly, "and you know it." How could he be so cool? He was made of ice.

"You're seriously telling me you expect me to have remained celibate at the age of thirty-four?" he asked incredulously.

"Not celibate, of course not," she answered

quickly. ''But from what I hear there's never been any danger of that and casual affairs aren't my style.

''From what you hear?'' He moved closer now and she saw his mouth was a thin straight line. ''And what exactly have you heard, my busy little bee?''

''This and that.'' The tautness of his body was frightening her and she turned with a flick of her head towards the direction of the house. ''I'm cold; I'm going back.''

''The hell you are,'' he said grimly as he jerked her round to face him again. ''Now, what have you heard and from whom?''

''It's common knowledge you like women, lots of women.'' The bruising grip on her arm was hurting but she wouldn't admit it for the world. ''Can you deny that?'' she asked desperately.

''Common knowledge?'' His lip curled away from his teeth and for a moment he resembled a huge black wolf preparing to pounce. ''You listen to gossip, is that it, and, more to the point, have the stupidity to believe it?''

''You *are* denying it?'' Her tone was caustic and her head high, but the weakness that was invading her limbs told her she wanted him to repudiate her words, badly.

''I wouldn't lower myself even to take such rubbish that far,'' he said cuttingly. ''If you listen to the gutter Press, Janie, you have to expect to be soiled by the contact.''

''But someone—'' She stopped abruptly. ''It was

on good authority," she finished weakly, her heart thudding.

"Well, I should be a little more discerning in my choice of company in the future, if I were you," he said derisively, his tone sharp and stinging. "I haven't been dead from the neck downwards regarding women since puberty, no, but neither have I been put out to stud, as you would seem to suggest. But that's my own affair, surely?" The blue eyes were devastatingly cold. "It's of no interest to you one way or the other, is it? That much you have made perfectly plain."

She stared at him for a second, utterly unable to reply as the realisation that she would never again meet anyone else like him seared through her brain. He took the word "arrogant' to a new dimension; he was cold, ruthless, seemingly without pity for those who fell foul of him, and yet— The question mark was back again stronger than ever. There were times when he was so different, fascinatingly sensual, warm, tender, gentle...

"Kane—"

"No more tonight, Janie. I really couldn't take any more without doing something we'd both regret. You have the dubious distinction of being the only woman I've ever met who has the ability to drive me to the very limit and that's precisely where I am now. In spite of the fact that it's several degrees below zero, the temptation to take you right here and now is fast becoming too strong to resist, but it would be the wrong time in more ways than one and to prove something you aren't ready to acknowledge yet."

"But—"

"Come on." He cut off further conversation by taking her hand in a grip that was far from gentle and almost hauling her along at his side as he strode back towards the house, his face grim and tight and his eyes looking straight ahead.

As she trotted along in an undignified jog all her energy was concentrated on not slipping on the icy ground and finding herself in a more ridiculous position than the present one, but later that night, in the safety of her room, as she snuggled deep into the huge bed, she wandered back and forth over their conversation until she was thoroughly confused and close to tears, and when Juniper joined her on the bed, his big, warm body vibrating with the miniature express train purring deep inside him, it was the final straw. The surprised cat found himself being held very tightly, his fur getting damper by the second as Janie cried herself to sleep in a way she hadn't done since she was a small child.

# CHAPTER SEVEN

BOXING DAY lunch was a cold buffet and as Janie helped herself from the laden table she found Tina at her side, the blonde's cool blue eyes sharp on Janie's face. "Quite well again, I see?" The tone was far from pleasant. "We're not used to such drama at Christmas. June tells me it was like a scene from an old movie when Kane carried you in Christmas Eve—a little waif and stray rescued by her dream hero."

"Hardly." Janie turned to face Tina, staring fully into the hard, beautiful face. "I'm no stray and Kane hasn't featured in any dreams that I've been aware of, and yes, I feel fine now." That was a lie, her legs felt peculiarly weak now and again and her head still had moments of leaving her body, but not for the world would she betray any weakness to the reptilian-like, unblinking eyes watching her so closely.

"This cool routine is very clever," Tina said conversationally as she followed Janie to the huge window-seat at the far end of the room, plate in hand. "It certainly seems to have him interested for the moment—men are so gullible."

"Are you always this unpleasant?" Janie asked directly, suddenly tiring of the other woman's cat-and-mouse game. "It's very boring."

"Really?" In spite of the chilly tone a surge of hot colour stained the high cheekbones red and Janie knew her remark had hit home. "Well, I do apologise for being tedious, darling, but then maybe you aren't used to the niceties of social intercourse? I understand you're a little secretary somewhere?" Tina raised one finely shaped eyebrow in quizzical contempt.

"I work for my living, if that's what you mean," Janie said quietly, "and thoroughly enjoy every minute. Does your life give you pleasure and fulfilment?" It was below the belt but she felt the other woman deserved it, and as Tina drew back with a tightening of her thin, well-shaped lips, her blue eyes narrowing, Janie saw her hands clench violently in her lap.

She'd like that to be my throat, Janie thought with a little shiver of dark amusement as the other woman leant forward again, her voice a low hiss.

"You think you're so clever, don't you, catching his eye and being invited for Christmas? Well, don't get any bright ideas, little Miss Know-it-all. He may be slumming for the moment, but you are just another fancy that will go the way of all the rest. You've got nothing that could hold him—"

"Why are you so concerned anyway?" Janie had wanted her voice to be cool and clear but the other woman's naked vindictiveness had turned her stomach. "Kane's personal life is absolutely nothing to do with you."

"That's what you think!" There was a note in Tina's voice, an obsessional intensity in her eyes that made Janie's flesh creep.

Just at that moment the object of their conversation appeared in the doorway, his eyes narrowing as he glanced across to the two women and saw the look on Janie's face. He had been closeted in his study since breakfast, much to his mother's disgust, Mrs Steel having made her objections very plain that morning. "Really, Kane, this is supposed to be a holiday," she had said disapprovingly as her son had excused himself from the walk the others were planning as they finished coffee in the breakfast-room. "Do you have to work?"

"Afraid so." He had glanced at Janie, the blue eyes guarded and distant. "Do you mind?" he'd asked expressionlessly.

"Me? Of course not," she'd answered, immediately earning a long sardonic look in the process that had made her heart thud uncomfortably.

"No, I thought not," he'd said drily, his meaning plain to her alone. "I'm afraid there's something that won't wait."

"The Collins deal?" His father's voice had been understanding and Kane had nodded quietly.

"Afraid so, but don't let me spoil the day." His eyes had flicked over the two small heads of the children, who were sitting finishing mugs of warm milk. "Enjoy the time with the kiddies; the pool's heated up like a hot bath, but perhaps you'd prefer to take them in this afternoon?"

His father had nodded slowly. "You can't save it, Kane," he'd said quietly. "Let it go, son. Give him a good price and leave it at that. You can't help Collins if John won't agree.''

"We'll see." Kane's voice had been curt and then he'd checked himself, his eyes softening as they glanced at the older man. "Enjoy your walk."

The memory of that conversation had bothered Janie all morning and now, as she caught Kane's eyes over the heads of the others, she saw that he was coming straight to where she sat.

"Getting to know each other?" he asked Tina, his eyes tight on the blonde's beautiful face, which was cool and superior again.

"Yes." His sister-in-law stood up gracefully, the faint smile touching the hard mouth as she glanced at his dark face dying instantly when she noticed the expression in the blue eyes. "I'll just help Aileen with the children."

"I shouldn't bother if I were you. She's used to looking after them on her own," Kane said grimly as he took Tina's arm when she made to walk away. "Please do continue the conversation you were having before I so rudely interrupted."

"It was nothing important; I really can't remember," Tina said coldly as her eyes flicked over his face. "Girl talk, you know…"

"Not really." Kane pressed her down on the window-seat with just enough force to let her know he meant business. "But perhaps you'd like to enlighten me?"

"We were just saying how lucky it was that you found me on Christmas Eve," Janie said lightly after a few heavy seconds had ticked by. Tina's face had slowly reddened, but it wasn't through any finer feelings towards the blonde that Janie stepped into the breach. She had seen Kane's mother glancing over at their little huddle several times in the last minute and knew the older lady sensed that something was wrong. Aileen had shown Janie nothing but kindness and she didn't want her upset.

"I see." Kane released his hand from Tina's shoulder as one of the children began to wail, clearly tired. "Well, maybe you'd better break the habit of a lifetime and see to the children, Tina," he said scathingly as he stepped back to let the blonde stand up. "And perhaps we'll have time to have a little chat later, eh?" It was a statement, not a question, and two pairs of blue eyes did vicious battle for a second.

As Tina disappeared, muttering something unpleasant under her breath, her face tight, Janie looked up at Kane warily. "How has your morning gone?" she asked lightly, her stomach muscles contracting as she took in the sheer attractiveness of the rugged face watching her so intently. The room had come alive as soon as he had entered it, she thought despairingly. She couldn't cope with all these emotions that were turning her upside-down—she just couldn't.

"Damn my morning," he said tightly as he sat by her side, the feel of his hard-muscled thigh against hers causing her heart to pound into her throat. "She was bothering you, wasn't she? The woman's a menace."

"I'm a big girl now." She couldn't bring herself to

look at him; the trembling that his presence had started in her body might be reflected in her eyes. "I can look after myself."

"Perhaps I don't want you to look after yourself," he said huskily. "Perhaps I want to take that job on."

"Don't." She closed her eyes for a moment, her heart racing. "Don't say things like that."

"Why not?" He took one of her hands and spread out her small fingers on his big palm. "Would that be so bad?"

"You know how I feel—"

He cut into her faltering voice abruptly, entwining her fingers tight in his.

"No. I know how you *try* to feel, but you're fighting something that's stronger than both of us. Trust me a little, Janie. Light a candle to banish the darkness; break the web."

"I can't." Her voice was a little moan. "Surely you can understand that I can't."

"You will." There was no triumph or violence in his voice, just a deep certainty that stirred the very depths of her being in spite of everything. She had the sudden crazy impulse, which had happened more than once lately, to rest her head on the broadness of his chest, to let him do what he would, to succumb to a will greater than her own; but that would be nothing short of suicide.

Tina's words bit starkly into her mind. "He may be slumming for the moment, but you are just another fancy that will go the way of all the rest." She had been being spiteful, but the words were an echo of the fears in Janie's own heart. He was a giant among men in more ways than one, rich, powerful, incredibly attractive. He would only want her for a short time and then he would expect her to disappear as gracefully as his other women, once the affair was over.

*But she wasn't made like that.* She almost moaned aloud. If she gave herself to him it would mean more than just a casual holiday diversion... The thought brought her abruptly back to sanity. Why was she thinking like this? Her father hadn't even featured in her anguish. How could she have forgotten the past?

"Let me get you a glass of wine." He stood up slowly, unaware of her turmoil, and as he walked across the room she noticed again a slight unsteadiness in his step that was immediately corrected. There had been numerous little instances like that all over Christmas, she thought suddenly as separate events slotted into the screen of her mind, a hundred and one occasions when the big body had almost seemed out of balance for a fleeting moment. She shrugged mentally; she was imagining things.

"Tell me a little about your job, Janie." Aileen had joined her, the older woman's kind eyes bright with genuine interest, and as Janie described her work Kane returned, listening intently as she talked. An hour crept by and as long as Janie kept reminding herself not to meet the ice-blue eyes that had the power to draw her inextricably close she could give the impression that she was quite composed and at ease when inwardly the very opposite was true.

"You're staying for the party, Janie?" Aileen asked

as they were finishing coffee in the drawing-room, the atmosphere a little easier since Tina had disappeared to her suite of rooms.

"Of course she is," Kane said calmly and distinctly as he took the two women's coffee-cups and placed them on the tray. "Although Janie doesn't know about it yet. We'll go for a drive if you like and I'll explain," he added, turning to Janie. He looked down at her, his eyes a pearly blue from the shafts of sunlight streaming into the room from the huge windows. "You'll be quite warm enough in the car."

"Oh, but you couldn't leave everyone," she said quickly.

"Nonsense," Aileen said heartily. "I heard George planning to use the pool this afternoon with the children and I think I intend to have a little nap. A nice relaxing drive will do you the world of good, Janie, and there's no need to hurry back. We all just eat when we feel like it on Boxing Day."

"A nice relaxing drive'? Janie smiled carefully at the older woman, determined not to meet Kane's eyes. There would be nothing relaxing about being alone with Kane in a confined space.

"There you are," Kane drawled mockingly as his mother wandered off with a beaming smile. "You have no excuse."

"I could say I just don't want to come," Janie said quietly, stiffening as he brushed an errant strand of hair off her cheek, the touch of his firm flesh sending a tingling through her skin.

"You could." He eyed her quizzically. "But you

aren't going to. An afternoon in Tina's company is more than flesh and blood could stand so I shall carry you out to the car by force if I have to.''

"We could swim," she said obstinately. "I haven't seen your indoor pool yet and—"

"The pool will keep." She flinched, sharply and abruptly, as he caught her hand, raising it to his mouth and kissing the soft skin lingeringly while he watched her with hard, glittering eyes. "We're going for a drive, Janie. Go and get your coat."

The weak sunshine held no warmth as they walked towards the garages a few minutes later, but the white light turned the sky a blindingly clear blue and the icy air was clean and invigorating considering they were situated on the outskirts of the nation's capital.

"You're driving?" she asked in surprise as she noticed the keys in his hand.

"You find that surprising?" He eyed her sardonically. "I did manage to get around before Baines was employed, you know. I even had a couple of motorbikes until—" He stopped abruptly. "Until a couple of years ago," he finished flatly.

"You decided your years of hell-raising were over?" she asked lightly and he nodded slowly, his eyes warm as they rested on her upturned face.

"Something like that."

It would be so easy to let him get under her skin, she thought helplessly as he opened the garage doors and disappeared in the nearest one. He made her feel fully alive for the first time in her life and the sensation was intoxicating as well as frightening. Did she *really* believe he had known about the circumstances involved in her father's demise? She shook her head despairingly as somewhere in the depths of the garage an engine roared into life. I don't know, she thought weakly, I really don't. She had never felt so muddled and bewildered in all her life.

For some reason, she had expected the Bentley to draw slowly out of the garage, but the sleek red Jaguar that suddenly leapt to her side was as far removed from its garage companion as it was possible to be.

"What a gorgeous car." As she slid into the front seat beside Kane she glanced at him quickly. "It must have cost you a fortune."

"It's an indulgence," he admitted with a slightly shamefaced grin that jerked at her heart-strings, "but when I got rid of the bikes I felt the need for speed on four wheels. It's the fastest production car in the world."

"It looks it." She smiled at the obvious pride on his face. "I'm impressed."

"It was worth it, then." There was a deepness in the dark voice that sent a little shiver flickering down her spine and she glanced out of the window hastily, her nerves jumping. If anyone had ever told her that the mere sound of a man's voice could do the strangest things to certain parts of her anatomy she would never have believed them, she thought wryly as the powerful car purred obediently down the long, winding drive. No wonder this car had appealed to him. They were two of a kind: arrogant, dangerous and with the ability to captivate and demand immediate homage.

Once on the main road outside the estate Kane veered sharply to the right, down a narrow winding lane that ran between the walls of his grounds and farm fields on the left, the sleek car growling with impatience at having to restrain its speed. The sky was beginning to turn a brilliant gold, the first faint flush of pink stealing across the wide expanse. "It's later than I thought." Kane glanced at her swiftly. "It's already turning dusk. There's a little country pub I know about twenty minutes away. Fancy calling in for a swift one?"

"Fine." Janie nodded without looking at him. The sensation of being in such a powerful, expensive car was taking a little getting used to. In fact this whole experience was more than a little mind-boggling. She cast a secret glance at him from under her lashes, and her heart pounded violently as she took in the dark profile. He was wearing a fur-lined black leather jacket and black driving gloves and the whole image of car and man blended together into pure unadulterated sensuality.

Tina's gibe flashed into her mind: "a little waif and stray rescued by her dream hero". Perhaps the other woman hadn't been far wrong, she reflected with dry self-mockery. You certainly didn't get many men like him shopping in the local supermarket or visiting the launderette on a Saturday night. She smiled to herself at the thought.

"Penny for them." She hadn't realised he was looking at her and she flushed guiltily.

"Oh, it was nothing," she prevaricated quickly.

"Janie, I can count on one hand the times I've seen you smile in my company," he said caustically. "You could at least tell me why on this occasion."

"Do you really want to know?" she asked warningly. "You might not like it."

"I don't doubt that for a second," he said flatly. "Come on, then, shoot."

"I was just wondering how often in your life you've visited the launderette." She felt a moment's ridiculous satisfaction at the look of amazement on his face. "That's all. You probably don't even know what one is, though," she added blandly, but with a touch of underlying sarcasm that he didn't miss.

"Quite a few times, as it happens." He drew abruptly into a small lay-by that overlooked a small village, the sun a golden ball in the distance, and switched off the engine as he turned to look at her. "I did do three years at university, you know, and then I took off round Europe for a couple of years, bumming around."

"But you had lots of money—"

"No." He stared at her hard. "I didn't want to be different from my particular group of friends and none of them had a dime. We used to sleep on the beaches, in the local doss-houses, you name it." The blue eyes twinkled wickedly at her amazement. "One of the less reputable establishments was even infested with fleas. Disgusting, as I remember," he added reflectively, his eyes looking inwards now. "But we had a great couple of years."

"Do you still see any of them now?" she asked

curiously, as he sat staring out into the winter afternoon, fascinated by this unexpected glimpse into his life.

"Uh-huh." The vivid blue eyes focused on her again. "Charlie and Ben are doctors now, both married. Mike's still bumming from one job to another—itchy feet—and Nathan's the original family man with a brood of six infants at the last count."

"Six?" She eyed him laughingly.

"They live in a little terraced house in the middle of Newcastle, where he's a vet, and it's bedlam," Kane said quietly with a look on his face she couldn't quite fathom. "It's also the happiest place on earth."

"Is it?" She stopped smiling as he nodded slowly, his eyes piercingly hypnotic on her face.

"They love each other, you see," he said softly. "The sort of love that comes once in a lifetime."

The air grew heavy and quiet and she sought desperately for a way to break the bond of intimacy that had crept into the stillness. "And that's all of them?"

"No." His voice changed and he turned away from her now, his profile tightening. "My best friend, John, is in America fighting desperately with all he possesses to save his father's business from the wolves. John Collins." He looked at her hard. "The trouble is, he won't accept favours that he can't repay and the damn fool is effectively tying my hands at the same time as his father is begging for help. Hell of a situation, isn't it?" He shook his head slowly. "Heads or tails, everyone loses. Look, can we leave this now?" His face was almost hostile as he fired the ignition, his mouth straight. "I'll tell you about it properly some time, but not now."

"Of course, I'm sorry," she said quietly as he swung out into the road again. "I didn't mean to pry."

He shrugged lightly. "You didn't." He glanced at her swiftly, his eyes softening. "I'm just not too good at baring my soul; it's not something I normally indulge in." The smile he gave her melted her bones. "Let's go and find that pub, shall we?"

I don't want this. I don't want this. The words were a persistent drumming refrain in her head as they drove slowly through the small village, which was nothing but a tiny cluster of houses grouped round the local post office and corner shop, and up a gradual incline on the other side, passing through a more heavily built-up area within minutes before turning once again into a winding country lane with fields either side in which placidly chewing bovines eyed the sleek car uninterestedly. Something was happening to her and it scared her to death. How soon could she decently make her escape? As though he had read her mind he spoke quietly into the silence that had fallen.

"The party my mother mentioned is just a small one to round off Christmas. You'll stay, of course?"

By enormous will-power she kept her voice cool and bland as she replied, her face expressionless, "I don't think so, thanks. I ought to be getting home. It was very kind of you—"

"Don't start all that again." Immediate colour flared into her face at his clipped tone.

"Don't start all what again?" she asked indignantly.

"The 'escape from the wolf's lair' routine," he said testily. "The party is on Sunday. Are you expected at work on Monday?"

"Yes." She wasn't sure if Joe expected her back then or not, but that was incidental.

"Then I will run you home afterwards," he said coolly.

"But I don't want to—"

"Dammit, Janie!" The bark was so sudden that she jumped visibly. "What the hell is the matter with you, girl? I'm asking you to stay for a party, not a session on the rack. At least do me the courtesy of *pretending* that all this isn't too repellent."

"It's not repellent," she said weakly as she noticed that his knuckles were white where his hands gripped the steering-wheel. "It's just that—" She stopped, unable to go on.

"Yes?" His tone was hardly conducive to further conversation.

She took a deep breath, her eyes cloudy with emotion. "It's just that I don't know what you expect of me," she said miserably after a long moment. "You know how I feel, about my father and everything. I just find it hard to…" She searched for the right words.

"Trust me?" he finished quietly, his eyes looking straight ahead.

"I suppose so." She didn't dare look at him now as they travelled through the dusk-filled evening, the sky a deep red against which the stark black outlines of the bare trees stood out in magnificent contrast.

"I didn't have any knowledge of it when it was happening, Janie, you can believe that," he said softly as they drew into the rough square of partly concreted land that was the pub car park. "I wouldn't lie to you about this."

After cutting the engine he leant back in his seat with one arm stretched along the back of hers, his blue eyes fixed on her troubled face. "Sooner or later you are going to have to take a few chances in life," he said softly after a full minute had passed. "Why not start now, with me? I'm not asking that you immediately declare undying devotion, Janie, just that you try and open your mind a little and take each day as it comes. Is that really too much to ask?"

"What were the papers you brought round Christmas Eve?" she asked suddenly. Somehow they were important to the present conversation although she wasn't sure why.

The piercing eyes didn't leave her face as he replied, his voice slow and steady, "Mostly a result of my investigations," he said softly. "There *was* an injustice done, but I hadn't realised at first how serious it was. The papers are documents that prove this and also detail the amount your father should have been paid. I want you to have the money, Janie—" He stopped abruptly as she moved in protest and he raised an authoritative hand quickly. "No, let me continue. Once it's paid to you you can do whatever you like with it—give it away to charity if you still consider it's blood money—but I want you to accept it.''

''Guilty conscience?'' she asked quietly.

He nodded agreement. ''As you said when we first met, the buck stops here. Whatever the circumstances, the transactions were made in the name of Steel Enterprises and that means I collect the cheque. I've never yet knowingly cheated someone out of their rightful due, and I wouldn't like to set a precedent with your father. I can't undo the damage that resulted, I can only repeat that I had nothing to do with it. You have to decide if you believe me and also if that's enough to set the candle flickering.''

''The candle?'' She stared at him mesmerised in the dim light from the dusky twilight that filled the silent car. The trembling his presence always induced was there at the pit of her stomach, the sensually delicious smell of him filled her nostrils, the overall dynamic power of the man seemed intensified a hundred times in the close confines of the car.

''The light to banish the darkness,'' he said softly.

''But why—?'' She stopped abruptly. What she had been about to say was very gauche.

''Why?''

Oh, blow it, she thought with a sudden surge of strength. She had to ask, however gauche it sounded. ''Why are you interested in me anyway? If you are,'' she added hastily as the cool face didn't change expression. ''I mean, the world is your oyster, after all, and the women you could choose—''

''Well, correct me if I'm wrong, but at the last look

I could have sworn *you* were a woman,'' he said, his smile holding a tinge of mockery. ''So why not you?''

''I'm not exactly your type, am I?'' she murmured quietly, her cheeks hot with embarrassment. ''I mean—''

''Who says you aren't my type?'' His voice was very thick and very deep and the butterflies in her stomach suddenly went crazy.

''Kane—''

''Come here.'' As her lips parted his mouth took possession of hers, the explorative power of his tongue sending a bolt of electricity down to her toes. She could kiss him forever, she thought with a tinge of horror as he locked her against him. She had never come across such pure evocative power in a mere kiss before. His hands came up to frame her face tenderly, his mouth still hard on hers, and then his lips began a devastatingly seductive wander over her cheeks, her eyelids, her ears, until she began to think she was going to melt at his feet.

''Now.'' He settled back in his seat again, one hand playing with her neck under its veil of silky black hair. ''Can you honestly tell me that you don't get a little inkling that I find you more than acceptable?'' The gleam of humour lighting the blue eyes played havoc with her jangled nerves. ''And for the moment you are going to do as you're told, Janie Gordon. We are going to go in the pub and have a cosy drink before dinner and then you are going to spend the rest of the evening devoting yourself exclusively to my company. Before long you are going to be like the rest of my women, falling down in adoration at my feet!'' The words were said with humour, a dry self-mockery apparent in every one, but as he repeated the remark she had flung at him earlier in anger a piercing bolt of lightning seemed to spear her in two as she admitted to herself that that was *exactly* what she had been fearing all along.

# CHAPTER EIGHT

SATURDAY passed in a rose-coloured daze that even Tina's subtle, poisonous remarks couldn't penetrate. I'm falling in love with him, Janie acknowledged later that night as she lay curled up in bed with Juniper and Cosmos at her side. It was against all reason, all logic, and she didn't want to but...she hugged her pillow tightly...she couldn't help it. Could she really love anyone she didn't trust? she asked herself some time later when sleep proved elusive. And did she trust him? She wriggled in the bed, to the annoyance of the two cats. She didn't know. She didn't know anything any more. One minute she wished she'd never met him and the next...

She remembered the long walk they'd gone on that afternoon in the crisp, clean air that was fragrant with woodsmoke and winter. The easy way they'd talked and laughed together, the love-making— She shivered suddenly and made a small anguished sound in her throat. She was probably the biggest fool on earth, but how could she be *sure*...?

June brought her a breakfast tray early on Sunday morning, her young face preoccupied and busy. "It's a right two and eight downstairs, miss," she said cheerfully as she pulled the curtains. "Mrs Langton's been up since five preparing for this party. You'd have thought we were having the Queen visiting, at least."

"Can I help at all?" Janie asked quickly.

"Good grief no, miss," June said, horror-stricken. "Mrs Langton'd have a blue fit. The caterers are down there at the moment doing this and that, but nothing is right as far as she's concerned. We're only having forty or so. I don't know why she's so concerned."

"Forty or so?" Janie asked as her heart sank. "I thought it was just a little party?"

"Well, it is, miss," June said bewilderedly. "There's been two hundred here before now when Mr Steel has felt like entertaining, especially in the summer with the gardens and all. Forty is nothing."

As soon as she'd finished breakfast Janie padded over to the wardrobe and looked dismally at her clothes. She'd worn the black dress and a chocolate-box cocktail dress here—they wouldn't do. Her eyes roved over the few good evening clothes Mrs Langton had packed. Maybe white silk trousers teamed with the sleeveless cut-away top she'd bought in Paris on a day trip last year? She hauled it out of the wardrobe and laid it on the bed. The sequinned top was dramatic in black and white, almost backless, with tiny shoulder-straps and a plunging neckline. That outfit would give anyone a run for their money, she thought approvingly as she eyed it on the bed. She didn't dwell on exactly whom. No doubt there would be more than a few model-slim shapes here tonight. And she'd have her hair down. She remembered Kane's hands as he'd played with her hair the afternoon before, his eyes hungry, and sat down on the bed with a small plop. This was crazy; *she* was crazy!

By the time the first guests had begun to arrive just before teatime, Janie had worked herself up into a state of brittle fatalism. This was probably all going to go wrong, she thought helplessly as the first person to walk through the door was the ethereal blonde she had seen Kane with at the Press conference. She'd been mad even to consider that he was serious about her.

"There you are." As Kane slipped a possessively firm arm round her waist she blinked up at him in surprise. "Sorry, I got delayed—phone call." He was devastatingly attractive in beautifully cut casual trousers and a pure silk shirt that sat on the big, hard chest like a delicious advertisement for the body beneath. She hadn't seen him for most of the afternoon; he had been closeted in the study again and she had determined from his father that he was still fighting out the Collins merger with father and son respectively.

"Successful phone call?" she asked lightly, trying to concentrate on anything but the feel of his hard thigh next to hers.

"Maybe, at last," he said slowly. "I've got the old man and John talking together now so perhaps we can reach some sort of compromise—joint partnership with Steel Enterprises—something along those lines. John's so damn proud..." He smiled sardonically. "And no comments about the male ego."

"I wouldn't dream of it," she said smoothly as the blonde walked by without him even noticing her.

"You're on edge. Don't be," he said a little while later, his gaze warm on her face. "You look beautiful, Janie. There's not a woman in the room who could compete with you."

"A little ungallant towards the rest of us, Kane?" Tina's face was smooth and smiling as she rested her hand lightly on his arm for a moment as she passed by in a swirl of black satin and flashing diamonds. Kane raised expressive black eyebrows in an expression of cynical amusement as they were joined by another couple but as Janie stared after the tall blonde she felt a little shiver snake down her spine. The woman was poison. Sheer poison. And never more so than when she was feigning refinement.

It wasn't until Janie was helping herself from the magnificent buffet that Tina sidled up to her, but she had felt the blonde's venomous hard gaze following her all night, the sapphire eyes glowing with hate. "I think Kane must have had every woman in this room at some time or other," the blonde's cultured, quiet voice said conversationally in Janie's right ear, "or at least those under thirty, anyway."

"I beg your pardon?" Janie had mentally prepared herself for some sort of onslaught, but the sheer vulgarity of the softly hissed words took her completely by surprise.

"It's amazing really, when you consider it," Tina continued smoothly, her eyes fixed on the food as she carefully filled her plate. "How he remains friends with them all afterwards. Still, he *is* quite an unusual man." She speared a piece of ham with her fork.

"Don't you think?" She glanced at Janie now, the narrowed eyes malevolent.

"I don't think this conversation—"

"Did you know I went out with him for a time, before Keith and I met, that is?" Tina cut through Janie's stiff voice with a voice of steel wrapped in silk. "So I do speak from experience, of course." She smiled meaningfully, her face vicious.

"Are you saying you slept with him?" Janie asked coldly as she met the other woman's flickering gaze head-on.

"Darling, how very direct of you," Tina drawled maliciously.

"Because if you are I would have to call you a liar," Janie said tightly, praying that the churning in her stomach wouldn't reveal itself in her voice. "I understand from Kane you met casually, three times, and that was the end of it." As Tina's eyes slid away from hers she took a step forward, her face composed and calm. "Would you like to tell me different?"

"Oh, it's all old history now, isn't it, darling?" Tina said slowly after a long moment of silence, her blue eyes narrowing into hard slits. "You don't want to know all the sordid details."

"You're pathetic, Tina." Janie's face was grim now and her eyes dark with dislike. "Pathetic and sick and twisted."

"How dare you?" The beautiful face was dark with a fiendish malevolence that turned Janie's stomach. "How *dare* you speak to me like that? I won't have it, I tell you—"

"And I won't listen to your lies and innuendoes," Janie said distinctly as she kept her voice cool and clear with tremendous effort. "Not now and not in the future."

"Future?" Tina's voice was shaking with rage. "Future? You seriously think you are going to have a future with Kane? And you have the nerve to call *me* pathetic! He won't stay with you; he won't stay with anyone, don't you see? He's a man, a proper man, the only one I've ever met, and he can't be caged by anyone. I see that—I know how he thinks; I can see what he needs…" It was the look of horror in Janie's eyes that brought the low, hissing voice to a halt a second before Kane's deep, cold voice spoke out behind Tina's tense body.

"Go to your room, Tina." As the blonde turned to face him Janie couldn't see the look on her face, but Kane's was terrible to behold. "And pack your things. Baines is taking you home."

"Kane—"

He cut off the whimper with a ferocious shake of his head. "*Now*, or so help me I won't be responsible for my actions."

"You can't do this to me, Kane." There was a strange note in Tina's voice now, almost a sing-song blandness that made Janie's flesh creep, and she realised, for the first time, the full enormity of what it must have meant to his brother to live with such a woman for so long. No wonder it had killed him. "I'm a part of your family whether you like it or not. You can't treat me like you treat the others."

"Come with me, Tina." He took her arm, leading her from the room with an expressionless face, and Janie felt shaky with relief that she had gone quietly, although the last long look Tina had sent in her direction had been heavy with vicious spite, and something else—a weird kind of sane madness.

It was a long time before Kane returned and already one or two of the guests had left, and in the ensuing leave-taking and effusive goodbyes there was no opportunity to speak privately with him.

It was as they were waving goodbye to the last guest from the doorway along with his parents that Kane spoke. "Tina's left, Mother." He turned to face Aileen directly as they stepped back into the hall and closed the front door.

"Left?" His mother stared at him in astonishment. "Tonight? Who with? And where are the children?"

"Upstairs, fast asleep," he said quietly. "Tina's father collected her. I understand they are planning some sort of world cruise and he suggested it might be a good idea for her to go along with them for the next few months. Her father feels she needs a break without the children and he knows they will be happy and secure with you. He's going to ring tomorrow to discuss details and tie up any loose ends."

"This is very sudden." His mother stared at him blankly. "But then I've never understood Tina and she isn't very maternal. Do you think the last twelve months have affected her more than she has said?" she asked her husband suddenly, her face guilt-stricken.

"I doubt it," George said drily, "but Tina doesn't divulge too much to anyone, does she? I think this is probably exactly what everyone needed. It will give us a break to sort things out," he added quietly after a long, hard glance at his son's grim face.

As he led his wife away he peered once over his shoulder, his eyes questioning, but Kane shook his head quickly, a finger on his lips. "See you tomorrow, Dad." The words were bland but his father nodded slowly, the unspoken message received and understood.

"Janie?" As his parents disappeared to their rooms Kane put his hand on her arm, his face grey with reaction. "I need to talk to you, to be with someone normal; do you mind?"

"Of course not." The naked pain in his eyes was heart-wrenching and, guided by instinct rather than her head, she reached up and pulled his face down to her lips, kissing him of her own volition for the first time before resting her head for a second against his hard chest.

"In here." He led her into his study, the fire a red glow in the dark room, kicking the door shut with the back of his foot as he pulled her immediately into his arms, his mouth hungry on hers. She knew what she was inviting as she kissed him back, but somehow nothing else mattered beyond bringing him comfort.

"I need you, Janie, so badly..." And as he spoke every sensitised nerve in her body responded to his husky groan. His hands urged her body more intimately against his, his breathing ragged and hoarse, his kiss deepening, and she knew she was lost. Lost in a mounting whirlwind that was taking all reasoning into its void, where nothing mattered but Kane.

They fell together on to the settee, limbs instinctively entwining as their mouths and hands sought for greater contact, and as her fingers slid inside his half-opened shirt he tensed for a second before capturing her mouth again. His body was hard and muscled and warm, the thick, curling body hair that covered the broad chest wonderfully erotic under her exploring fingers.

His own hands moved down the length of her back, slowly and caressingly, before slipping inside the thin top and feeling the silky satin of her skin. His lips were thrilling and tormentingly teasing in turn as he lowered his head to her throat and beyond to the soft swell of her firm breasts. "Janie, you're driving me mad…"

As their lovemaking reached new heights the pleasure that swept through her body was almost unbearable, and then he pulled away a little, levering himself up on his hands as he lay crouched over her, his eyes brilliant in the light from the fire. "I want you, Janie. *Now*, properly…" The dark face melted into the shadows of the room, the glittering eyes the only thing she could focus on. "Do you understand me?"

As reality washed in on a tidal wave of cold awareness she recognised, in one blindingly clear moment, that he had consciously given her the choice. He was experienced, versed in all the responses. He knew she had been his for the taking, but he had drawn back and purposely given her the choice. Why? *Why*? And suddenly, unreasonably, she felt blind panic.

"Kane, this is all happening too fast..." As she struggled to sit up he was completely still for one long, tense moment before sliding off the settee and walking over to stand in front of the dying fire, his back to her. "I'm sorry, really..." She took a deep breath at the rigid back. "I just don't know how I feel any more, what I really want," she finished on a little sob.

"I know exactly what I want." As he turned round very slowly she couldn't see his face in the shadows, just his black outline, big and menacing against the glow from the red coals. "More than at any time in my life."

There was a long, deep moment of screaming silence before she brushed her hand across her eyes, feeling impossibly close to tears. "I'm sorry," she whispered again, her voice shaking in spite of all her efforts to control it. "I didn't mean for things to get out of hand like that."

"Neither did I." His voice was low and soft. "But when I'm around you 'things' just tend to happen, don't they?" The mocking humour hurt a little and she realised, with a tiny jolt of self-disgust, that she wanted him to feel as desperate as she did at this moment, wanted him to sweep all her objections aside, wanted him to consummate their relationship in the age-old way. Her inconsistency caused a burning flood of humiliation to colour her cheeks scarlet.

"Will you take me home?" she asked in a small voice.

"If you promise to have dinner with me tomorrow night," he said immediately, his voice warm and steady.

"Would Tuesday do?" she asked as her heart hammered against her chest. "I need to get the flat sorted, wash my hair, the usual things..."

"So be it." The deep voice sent shivers trickling down her spine as his maleness made her hands damp. How could she want him as badly as this? When had this feeling overtaken her so completely? Where had all the cold logic and reasoning gone?

Baines had already loaded her luggage into the back of the Bentley, which was parked in the drive, waiting patiently under a full round moon that turned the paintwork into pure silver. Kane climbed into the front seat after settling her on the passenger side beside him. "Not as seductive as the Jag," he murmured with mocking humour as he started the powerful engine, "but maybe that's just as well tonight."

She wanted to treat the whole matter as lightly as he seemed to be able to do, but there was a huge restriction in the base of her throat that was making it difficult. If he hadn't stopped, right now she would be feeling very differently. She shut her eyes tightly for a second. Whether it would have been better or worse she was past knowing at the moment; he was still too close for coherent thought.

The big car moved swiftly through the beautiful moonlit night, the roads almost deserted at two o'clock in the morning, and as she remembered her journey down here just four days earlier she couldn't believe how totally he had taken over her thoughts and emotions, how completely he had annihilated every defence. And she was still so far from even beginning to understand what made him tick, even what sort of person he really was. Did she trust her head or her heart? The empty streets gave her no help to sort out a reply.

"Here we are." As he drew up outside the house she stared at him for a moment in the dim light, taking in each harsh feature, each line of his face, as though she would never see it again. This man had turned her life upside-down in just a few days, but the most terrifying thing was, she couldn't imagine the possibility of never seeing him again.

"I'm glad you wore it tonight." He touched her throat in a light gesture as he brushed the pendant with the tip of one finger. "Its power to catalyse is undiminished."

"I don't understand." She stared at him before nodding quickly. "Oh, you mean Tina."

"Not exactly," he said drily.

"She's going away?" It was suddenly much safer to concentrate on his sister-in-law. "Leaving the children?"

"Yes." He sighed harshly as he turned to look out through the windscreen. "Her father was more understanding than I could have hoped. It appears he loves her in spite of herself rather than wearing the rose-coloured spectacles I'd assumed were firmly in place. He liked Keith, he made that clear, and I think he'd got a pretty good idea of how the land lay. He's planning to be away for twelve months, perhaps even longer, and we'll make it official in due course regarding the children. Tina has never had any time for them; she can barely stand having them around at times. My mother is the mother they should have had.''

"Tina will agree to that?" Janie asked in amazement. "Her own children?"

"When a mother shark gives birth to her young they are perfectly formed in their own little sacks with umbilical cord attached, just like human offspring," Kane said in a hard, painful voice. "The second they are out in the ocean they are on their own—I mean really on their own—she has nothing more to do with them. Occasionally, very occasionally, nature plays a macabre joke and fashions its own walking shark on two legs. Enter Tina." He eyed her soberly. "There is nothing natural about the woman in any way, Janie. She has neglected them, ignored them, since they were born. Keith nearly went mad for a time until he accepted that, like everything else. He became mother and father to them and, of course, my mother helped.''

"How did he die, Kane?" She had never felt she could ask before, but here, in the darkness, time seemed suspended and unreal.

"Car accident," he said briefly. "The circumstances were odd. He apparently drove straight at a brick wall and there were no tyre marks to indicate that he swerved for any reason, but it was midnight on a deserted road with no witnesses." He shrugged flatly. "It was easier to let my mother believe it was an accident."

"You think suicide?" she asked, horror-stricken.

He nodded slowly. "Tina had turned him into the sort of man he loathed, Janie," he said tiredly. "He'd done things, said things that had seared his soul and still she wasn't satisfied. He was weak, he knew it, and he paid the ultimate price." He turned to her suddenly, taking her lips in a hard, fierce kiss that stopped her breath. "Are you sure you can wait two whole days before you see me again?" he asked softly as he took her face in his hands. She accepted the change of conversation without comment. Sometimes talking about her father had proved too painful after a time, especially in the early days when the bitterness had reached out to claw her stomach until she felt actual nausea. No wonder he loathed Tina with such intensity.

"I'll try," she said lightly as she opened the car door and climbed out into the frosty night. If she stayed in there another minute she'd be asking him to turn the car round and take her home with him again, home to his bed!

"Foolish girl..." He followed her to the front door, taking her in his arms again before she could protest and kissing her until the breath left her body. "Open the door," he said coolly when he eventually released her, hot and shaking. She eyed him furiously. How could he be so...irritatingly *imperturbable*?

"You needn't come up," she protested quickly as

he followed her into the small hall. "There's no need—"

"You've been away for four days and the house has been empty," he said calmly, totally unruffled. "I shall check you're OK and then vanish, unless you'd like me to warm your cold bed?" he asked wickedly.

By the time he left her nerves were stretched as tight as piano wire and she had never felt so confused in all her life, the sense of relief she felt as his footsteps disappeared down the stairs only matched by the surge of stunningly painful regret at his departure.

The flat was like an ice-box and as she lay shivering in bed a few minutes later, missing the warm bodies of Juniper and Cosmos more than she would have thought possible, she knew she was going to cry herself to sleep.

# CHAPTER NINE

WORK the next day proved to be an unmitigated disaster of the highest proportions, with Janie making the most elementary mistakes time and time again. By the end of the day she knew it was only the fact that Joe thought she was still suffering from flu that prevented him coming out with all guns firing.

"I'd take another couple of days off, Janie," he said quietly as she slipped into her coat that night, forcing a note of concern into his voice even as his eyes swept over another report she had got all wrong. "You aren't yourself yet."

I'll never be myself again, she thought silently as she nodded a reply and picked up her bag from the floor. I don't even know what myself is any more. "Thanks, Joe." She waved briefly from the doorway as she left. "Sorry about the mess I've made of things today."

Once home, she switched on the small gas fire in the pocket-size lounge, made herself tea and toast, and then sat warming her toes in front of the red heat as she ate. She washed her hair, cleaned the tiny flat from top to bottom, but still the restless energy that had her stomach churning and her hands shaking all day hadn't abated. And she wasn't seeing Kane till tomorrow.

"I need to *do* something," she told herself irritably after flicking through the channels of her small TV aimlessly. Her father's papers. She grasped the thought quickly. Kane's intention to refund the money he felt she was owed necessitated a careful check over the financial side of the transaction some time. She felt uncomfortable accepting anything at all and with the emotion that seemed to have developed between them he might just prove over-generous, which she couldn't bear.

Did she feel strong enough to dig out that box with all its painful reminders of her father's anguish and her own desperation? She sat back on her heels on the carpet in front of the small TV. Amazingly, yes, she did. She sat there for long minutes as, for the first time in two years, a kind of peace stole into her heart, blanketing the hurt and sorrow with a slow acceptance of what she couldn't change. She had to let go, had to reach out, had to trust what her heart was saying. The bitterness she had felt for so many months had been directed at a distant giant, an all-powerful dictator with the capacity for acts of brutal cruelty and heartlessness, but now... Now she knew Kane. And she loved him.

How long she sat in the quiet of her small lounge absorbing the knowledge that she had been fighting for days she didn't know, but when at last she stood up and fetched the box of papers the revelation had become fact. She didn't know what the future would hold—he had spoken no words of love, after all, and his world wasn't her world—but still she wanted to be with him for as long as he wanted her. The raw heart-ache he felt over his brother's death, his compassion and understanding over the Collins deal both for his best friend and John's father, his concern for his mother, his love of Keith's children... This wasn't a man who could callously cheat a middle-aged man out of his life's work and walk away without a backward glance. She believed that; she *had* to believe it.

She brushed a strand of black hair off her face as she thought back over the last few days. The amazingly tender private side that he had shown to her more and more when they were alone had been everything she could have wanted in a man, his strength not the brutal kind that so many men thought was macho and cool, but the sort that could have her walking into any situation with him, any circumstances, knowing that he would protect her at the cost of his own safety. She couldn't doubt his integrity any more, wouldn't.

Her thoughts winged back to the night before and the lovemaking that had been on a different plane from anything she had dreamed possible. It would have been the easiest thing in the world for him to have taken her at that moment; she had been helpless and willing beneath his body, utterly yielding to his male domination. But he had stopped.

She breathed hard in the still room. He didn't want just her body, he wanted all of her, she knew it. But where would that leave her when it ended, *if* it ended? How would she cope with the aftermath, the rest of her life?

His words came back to her as clearly as though he

were in the room with her. "Sooner or later you are going to have to take a few chances in life. Why not start now, with me?"

Yes, why not, Kane? she told him silently as she glanced round the small room. She wasn't going to fear the unknown any more but face it head-on, with him, and maybe…she shook her head slowly…just maybe he would grow to really love her?

After shaking off a large, dead spider and a network of filmy cobwebs, she emptied the papers on to the carpet and began to sort them methodically into date order. The heap was daunting but she had all evening and once the pile was established she sat back and began to read each one, making the odd note as she did so.

Her father had put up quite a fight. Several of the papers were smeared with tears before she was half-way through. He hadn't begged, he hadn't threatened, he had been courteous throughout, but the British bull-dog had reared its head and sunk its teeth in deep to what it owned.

After several cups of black coffee she only had a few papers left. She glanced at her notes and sighed softly. The financial reimbursement was considerable. Did Kane know? She shook her head slowly. He could afford it but she didn't want his money. It somehow seemed unfair although that was against all logic.

One o'clock in the morning. She glanced at her watch and decided to flick quickly through the few remaining papers before going to bed. She felt she could sleep now. The letter that sent her mind spinning into a deep black void was the third letter from the bottom and one she had never noticed before. She read it through quickly, then again more slowly, as her heart pounded so hard, she felt she was going to die, then a third time, as the letters on the page became imprinted in her mind in burning-hot weals. The typewriter used was one that printed a beautifully flowing italic print that yelled wealth and power.

Dear Mr Gordon,
It is always painful to put a time limit on negotiations of a delicate nature such as ours, but I feel Steel Enterprises can accept no more delay. Your procrastination has already lost you a considerable financial reward and I feel our offer is most generous in the somewhat desperate circumstances in which you presently find yourself. If you do not accept our terms and conditions for the take-over of your company within forty-eight hours, Steel Enterprises will withdraw from the transaction. Our knowledge of your financial difficulties would suggest that your position would then become untenable. It is always a sad and humiliating experience for a family name to suffer the indignity of court proceedings and I would like you to take this into consideration in your decision.

The usual official wind-up to such a letter followed, but it was the signature at the bottom of the thick bond paper that caused a harsh, raw ache in Janie's chest.

"K. Steel". A flowing, bold signature. And under-neath: "Chairman and Managing Director".

That was it, then. She raised her head and stared blindly at the opposite wall. He *had* known. *He had known*! Even if he hadn't been a party to the subtle pressure that had dropped the price to a third of the original offer over a period of months as her father had held out, and bribed or forced or coerced banks and other institutions to pull out the proverbial rugs from under her father's shaky feet. Even if he hadn't instigated all that, this letter proved that, in the final analysis, he had approved his employees' methods. And he wouldn't sign a letter like this without know-ing the full history of the transaction. Not he, not Kane Steel.

Janie didn't cry. She got ready for bed automatically and lay, eyes wide open, until dawn lightened the bed-room and the new day began. She felt numb, dead; the very essence of her had died and shrivelled away— she was nothing now. How could she have been so stupid? How could she?

She didn't go into work—she couldn't have func-tioned at all—and the day dragged by, hour by hour, minute by minute. Tomorrow was New Year's Eve. She'd had such hopes for this new year. She shut her eyes tight as, for a second, pain, hot and searing, broke through the ice round her heart and brought her hands round her middle in a tight hug while she swayed back and forth in the slowly darkening room. She wouldn't think now. Mustn't. He would be here in the next hour, and after that... The shudder that racked her body chilled her soul.

When his knock came she walked across and opened the door slowly, like an old woman, and as he caught sight of her white face his own grin of welcome died swiftly.

"What is it?" He threw down the huge bouquet of roses he had been holding as he followed her into the flat. "What on earth's happened?"

"I found a letter." Her voice, when it had been forced past the blockage in her throat, sounded almost normal, she thought with a strange detachment. The first sight of him had jolted her so badly, she had felt faint for a moment, but now, for the first time since she had found the letter, a savage, hot anger was bubbling inside her, strengthening her limbs and enabling her to turn and look at him without breaking down.

"A letter?" He looked at her blankly. "What sort of letter? Janie—"

As he reached out to her she stepped back so sharply, her neck snapped. "Would you like to read the letter?" she asked, her voice bitingly clear. "I think you should."

He remained stock-still as she walked over to the box in the corner of the room and lifted the letter from the top of the papers. "Here."

He took it from her, careful not to touch her hand, and glanced down the page swiftly, his face tightening as he did so.

"Well?" Her voice was too shrill and she took a

deep breath before she tried again. "Is that your signature?"

"I can explain this, Janie." As he met her eyes she saw a misery in his that was reflected suddenly in hers.

"How could you lie to me like that, Kane?" She had a sudden, fierce impulse to throw herself on him and claw his face to ribbons. "How could you pretend you were so innocent when all this time—?"

"I was." He took another step towards her, but she backed away from him, her cheeks burning. "Listen to me, please."

"Don't touch me, Kane. I'll kill you if you touch me."

"Listen to me, Janie—"

"I don't want to listen to you any more!" She was screaming now, the anger so intense, there was actually a red mist before her eyes. "I don't want to hear any more lies! Do you hear me?"

"I think the whole house can hear you," he said angrily as a flush of red stained his high cheekbones and his eyes chilled. "I can appreciate how this seems to you, but there is a good reason for it. If you'd just stop hollering long enough—"

"I hate you! I hate you!" When she flew at him it took all his strength to hold her at arm's length as she fought and kicked with her arms and legs, the bitter rage that swamped her body giving her superhuman power. After long minutes she sank down slowly on to the carpet, still flailing out at him as she did so, utterly spent.

"Are you going to listen to me now?" He stood

looking down at her, his face drawn and grim as dark emotion made his eyes almost black. "Give me a chance to explain?"

"I've listened to you enough," she said slowly. "No wonder you wanted to give me some money—I can see it all now—and to think that I felt guilty about considering accepting anything from you. Well, I *don't* want your money, Kane Steel; I don't want anything from you!"

Her voice had risen to a shout again and he shook his head slowly, his face grey. "I can't talk to you when you're like this," he said quietly. "Now, calm down."

"Calm down?" It was fuel for the fire and it burnt hotly. "How dare you say that? You're a liar and a cheat and I can see why Tina is so mentally unbalanced if she had anything to do with your family for long." It was below the belt and she knew it, regretting the spiteful, cruel words as soon as they were voiced, but she glared at him defiantly, determined not to weaken.

"This is doing neither of us any good," he said coldly, his eyes turning into chips of steel as he turned and walked towards the door. "I'll return when you are in control of yourself."

"Don't bother!" He paused, his body stiffening as she spat the words after him, and then carried on to the front door.

"Maybe I won't, at that." His voice was icy cold as the door shut. He'd gone? She pulled herself upright and crept into the easy-chair in front of the fire, her head spinning. He'd really gone? Well, she was glad, *glad*! If she ever saw him again in her life it would be too soon.

The deluge of tears took her completely by surprise but, once started, she found them impossible to stop. Every time she thought she had gained control, a fresh flood had her eyes streaming and her face wet, and at last she crawled into bed with a cup of cocoa and a hot-water bottle and lay in the darkness feeling utterly spent.

She hadn't expected to sleep, but the sleepless night the night before, and the trauma and emotion of the last twenty-four hours, had taken its toll so that when she next opened her eyes bright, cold sunlight was streaming into the room through a chink in the curtains. She lay for a moment in the drowsy warmth, wondering what the big black shadow was that had blanketed her mind—and then she remembered.

The bathroom mirror revealed a blotched white face and eyes swollen to such a degree, she felt she was peering out at the world through tiny slits. She felt a little better after a long warm shower, but only a little, and then, as she was fixing breakfast, the tears started again.

"Pull yourself together, Janie." She spoke out loud into the empty room. "You can't carry on like this— you look such a mess..." The day was worse than the one before; at least then she had been frozen into a weird kind of vacuum, just waiting for him to arrive with her mind cold and stunned and her brain ice-bound. Now the tears erupted every few minutes and it frightened her that she couldn't control them. She'd never felt like this before in her life, not even when her father died, and she had thought for a time then that she had reached rock-bottom.

I loathe him, I detest him, she thought later that morning as she went for a walk in the cold drizzle outside, looking aimlessly in shop windows and watching the rest of the world scurrying about in the way they always did in London, quite unaware that one of their fellow human beings was hurting. So why, if she felt like that, did she love him so much too? The thought caused her to stop dead in the street, her stomach somersaulting. She didn't, she *didn't*, but even as she fought against the debilitating knowledge she knew it was the truth. She loved him, helplessly, hopelessly, and it was beyond her power to turn the feeling off.

She walked through to one of London's tiny squares of green park, edged by railings, and sat on the wet wooden seat looking at the drooping greenery blindly. She hadn't listened to him, hadn't let him even offer an excuse... Could there be an explanation for it all? She shook her head slowly. Only the one, she had concluded. She couldn't live in hope of anything else. Maybe he regretted it bitterly; maybe he had buried the mean act so deep, he couldn't bring it to the sur-face... Stop kidding yourself, she thought angrily after a long time had dragged past. He had known what he was doing. But she hadn't listened. If he came back— *if*—she would hear him out, if only to exorcise the ghost. But she had lost him, whichever way things went; she had lost him and she knew, suddenly, that with the loss of Kane went a million and one other things she had always anticipated for the future. Marriage, children, her own family home shared with the man she loved. But he'd ruined all that, right from the day they'd met, because marriage couldn't possibly have featured in his scheme of things even if this bombshell hadn't fallen. And, after knowing him, no other man would do.

She had just thrown the meal she'd cooked for herself untouched into the bin when his knock sounded at the door. She knew it was him.

She opened the door slowly and looked up to see him staring down at her warily, his face tired and strained. "Can I come in?" he asked quietly.

She moved aside without speaking and walked back into the flat, hearing him shut the door behind him as he followed her into the tiny lounge. "If I begin to talk, explain, will you promise me not to say a word until I've finished?" he asked softly as she sat down on the chair, her eyes fixed on his face.

"All right." She indicated the other easy-chair with a wave of her hand but he shook his head slowly, the touches of silver above his ears glinting in the artificial light and causing an ache in her chest that suddenly gripped her with a terrifying intensity. She mustn't cry now, she *mustn't*, she told herself fiercely; she had to control herself. This was probably going to be the last time she ever saw him and it had to end with some sort of dignity.

"The signature on the letter is that of K. Steel," Kane said tightly as he began to pace the small room, his hands thrust deep into his pockets and his big body stooped slightly as though he was in pain. "And that's right." He looked at her for a split-second and she met his eyes steadily even as her whole being cried out against what he was saying. "But it was Keith Steel, not Kane, Janie." He had stopped for a brief moment, but now the pacing began again and she found herself almost unable to take in what he was saying, she was listening so hard through the pounding in her ears.

"Two years ago my brother stepped in and looked after my business for me for almost twelve months and I gave him complete authority in every area. I knew I could trust him; he loved me as much as I loved him, and he was the only person at that time I had confidence in and who knew the bones of everything. He was going through hell at the time with Tina, and it was probably the worst possible time for him to do it, but it was necessary and he insisted."

He stopped the pacing again and looked straight at her. "By the time I took the reins again other matters were in the front line and your father's firm was merely a name on a list I was given regarding acquisition. Can you believe that?" She nodded dumbly, the breathtaking relief and surge of joy she had felt at his explanation stilled by the look on his face.

"When I met you that first night I didn't know what to think at first, whether you were throwing some publicity stunt for one of my less noble competitors or for darker motives of your own, even if there was a grain of truth in your amazing accusations. And I was furious, raging mad. I wanted revenge and I intended to have it. But, from the moment I held you in my arms when you cried, I knew you, at least, thought your story was accurate and that was when the first little seed of suspicion was planted. My investigations confirmed my worst fears.

"I loved my brother, Janie." There was a note of something almost like bewilderment in his strained voice and, as she went to rise to go to him, he waved her back down, his expression suddenly tight.

"No. I have to finish this. I didn't want you to know it was Keith who had destroyed your father's business and his life—partly because he was my brother and I loved him, partly because he would never have acted like that if Tina hadn't screwed him up to the point where his whole life was geared to trying to prove himself ruthless, hard, dynamic, whatever you want to call it, and partly because—" He stopped abruptly, turning from her and walking across to the high, narrow little window that looked out on to the cold street, staring down into the darkness with his back to her. "Because I'd fallen in love with you that first night and I thought if you knew my family were responsible for destroying yours there would be no chance for us at all. When I told you about Keith killing himself I intended to complete the story and tell you it was because of mistakes he'd made like the one with your father, but I couldn't." The big figure hunched over. "It would have been as if I was killing all I'd got left of my kid brother, betraying him. I can't explain it, and it was partly my fault, too.''

''Your fault?'' She went to him now, turning him round to face her and looking up into his face, noticing as she did so that the blue eyes were glittering with unshed tears.

''Kane...'' She hugged him tight, reaching up to draw his face down to hers, but he stopped her quickly, pushing her away gently but firmly and walking across the other side of the room, as if to put space between them.

''I haven't finished, Janie.'' The note in his voice froze her instinctive impulse to rush across and fling herself into his arms, and she stared at him, her eyes wide with apprehension. ''It *was* partly my fault,'' he said slowly. ''I'd introduced Keith to Tina in the first place. I knew she married him when she believed, in a twisted, sick way, she loved me, but I couldn't tell him.'' His eyes were anguished. ''I just couldn't. I thought she'd grow to love him, appreciate the man he was. If I'd known the misery she was going to cause I'd have acted differently, but by then it was far, far too late. I didn't tell him because I didn't want to lose his love, and that was wrong—I have to live with that.''

''But how could you have known?'' she asked softly. ''How could anyone normal imagine a mind like Tina's? She's sick, Kane, really sick.''

''Janie, did I get it wrong with us?'' he asked abruptly, his eyes desperate. ''I need to know the truth. Were you beginning to care about me?''

"I do care, Kane," she said softly. "More than—"

"There's something else you must know." He had stopped her admission with such a savage gesture that she shrank back from him, her heart pounding. "The reason Keith took over the business was to help me." He eyed her painfully. "His own career had failed because he'd been too easy, too kind, and Tina never let him forget it for a second. I should have known he'd over-compensate, but it was a gamble I took, and we all lost. The only excuse I have is that at the time I was too ill to assess things properly."

"Ill?" She stared at him in amazement. Kane ill? He was so big, so strong, so formidable. Other people could be ill, but Kane?

"I had a major skiing accident two years ago that left me paralysed," he said expressionlessly, only his eyes betraying the horror of it all. "There was an op that had a fifty-fifty chance of success—heads I won, tails I didn't come through at all—and if it was a success it meant physio for years and a certain degree of pain for the rest of my life."

"Kane..." Her legs were trembling so violently, she had to sink down on the chair. Those touches of silver in his thick hair, the deep lines that had bitten into his flesh, the loss of balance she had noticed time and time again—it all fitted.

"I've a hell of a scar down my spine, Janie, so if you're squeamish now's the time to tell me," he said grimly as his eyes roved over her white face. "But before you do, let me tell you something. That crazy merry-go-round I'd been on? It all slotted into place as I lay there unable to move for days and weeks, and I had to face the fact that I'd made a hell of a mess of my personal life up to that point. I was rich and successful and everything I touched turned to gold, but I'd got nothing that meant anything in the final analysis. Do you know how that feels? I looked back over the women I'd known and there wasn't one I could have contemplated spending a week with, let alone the rest of my life, but I realised I needed someone who was totally mine, that I'd needed that for a long time without knowing it. But—'' he shrugged slowly ''—I didn't strike gold. Until one night four weeks ago, when a small brunette with eyes of fire accused me of murder and slapped my face in front of half the world.''

"Kane—'' She still couldn't move. It was too much. She'd been handed heaven on earth and it was just too much.

"The irony of it is, the girl I fell in love with that night loathed the very ground I walked on, and there were more obstacles than even I could deal with. I don't know how you really feel, Janie, but if there's a chance, however slim, tell me.'' The last words were a groan and now she moved, flying to his arms with a little moan of wonder.

"I want it all, Janie.'' He moved her back slightly to look down into her face and she saw that the doubt was still there. "I want to marry you. It has to be me and no one else, not ever, you understand me? And I'll never be able to dance the night away again—''

"I can think of better things to do than that to pass

the night away,'' she said softly, her face alight with
the force of her love as she reached up and traced the
harsh outline of his mouth.

A long, shuddering sigh that seemed to come from
the very depths of him passed into her and then he
took her mouth in a scorching kiss that told of his
hunger more adequately than words.

''I love you, Janie.'' He looked down at her, his
eyes glittering with fierce passion. ''I have from that
first night; that was what I was trying to tell you when
I gave you my grandmother's necklace. I love you,
adore you; you're all I've ever wanted and more. I
shan't be able to keep my hands off you; will you
mind?''

''I'm not sure.'' She raised starry eyes to his, her
mouth smiling. ''Perhaps you'd better show me what
you mean and then I'll tell you.''

So he did.

The world's bestselling romance series.

**HARLEQUIN®**
*Presents*

**Seduction and Passion Guaranteed!**

# GREEK TYCOONS

## They're the men who have everything— except a bride...

Wealth, power, charm—what else could a
heart-stoppingly handsome tycoon need? In the
GREEK TYCOONS miniseries you have already
been introduced to some gorgeous Greek
multimillionaires who are in need of wives.

Bestselling author *Jacqueline Baird* presents

### THE GREEK TYCOON'S REVENGE
Harlequin Presents, #2266
Available in August

Marcus had found Eloise and he wants revenge—by
making Eloise his mistress for one year!

This tycoon has met his match, and he's decided he *has* to
have her...*whatever* that takes!

**Pick up a Harlequin Presents® novel and you will
enter a world of spine-tingling passion and
provocative, tantalizing romance!**

**HARLEQUIN®**
*Makes any time special* ®

*Available wherever
Harlequin books
are sold.*

The world's bestselling romance series.

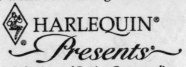

## HARLEQUIN®
### Presents

**Seduction and Passion Guaranteed!**

A new trilogy by **Carole Mortimer**

BACHELOR
COUSINS

## Three cousins of Scottish descent...they're male, millionaires and marriageable!

Meet Logan, Fergus and Brice, three tall, dark, handsome men about town. They've made their millions in London, but their hearts belong to the heather-clad hills of their grandfather McDonald's Scottish estate.

Logan, Fergus and Brice are about to give up their keenly fought-for bachelor status for three wonderful women—laugh, cry and read all about their trials and tribulations in their pursuit of love.

**To Marry McKenzie**
On-sale July, #2261

Look out for:
**To Marry McCloud**
On-sale August, #2267

**To Marry McAllister**
On-sale September, #2273

## Pick up a Harlequin Presents novel and you will enter a world of spine-tingling passion and provocative, tantalizing romance!

The world's bestselling romance series.

**HARLEQUIN®**
*Presents*

**Seduction and Passion Guaranteed!**

# SOCIETY WEDDINGS

**They're gorgeous, they're glamorous...
and they're getting married!**

Be our VIP guest at two of the most-talked-about
weddings of the decade—lavish ceremonies where the
cream of society gather to celebrate these marriages
in dazzling international settings.

Welcome to the sensuous, scandalous world
of the rich, royal and renowned!

SOCIETY WEDDINGS
Two original short stories in one volume:

**Promised to the Sheikh**
by *Sharon Kendrick*

**The Duke's Secret Wife**
by *Kate Walker*
on sale August, #2268

**Pick up a Harlequin Presents® novel and you will
enter a world of spine-tingling passion and
provocative, tantalizing romance!**

**HARLEQUIN®**
*Makes any time special®*

*Available wherever
Harlequin books
are sold.*

# Coming
# Next Month...

## A special promotion from

**Seduction and Passion Guaranteed!**

Details to follow in September 2002
Harlequin Presents books.

## Don't miss it!

Harlequin is proud to have published
more than 75 novels by

# Emma Darcy

Award-
winning Australian
author **Emma Darcy** is a
unique voice in Harlequin
Presents®. Her compelling, sexy,
intensely emotional novels have
gripped the imagination of readers
around the globe, and she's sold
nearly 60 million books
worldwide.

## Praise for Emma Darcy:

**Look out for more thrilling stories by Emma Darcy,
coming soon in**

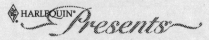